MW00412329

Whistling

and Other Stories

To the nuclear
editor and a
good citizen
of this wicked
world,
Best wishes.

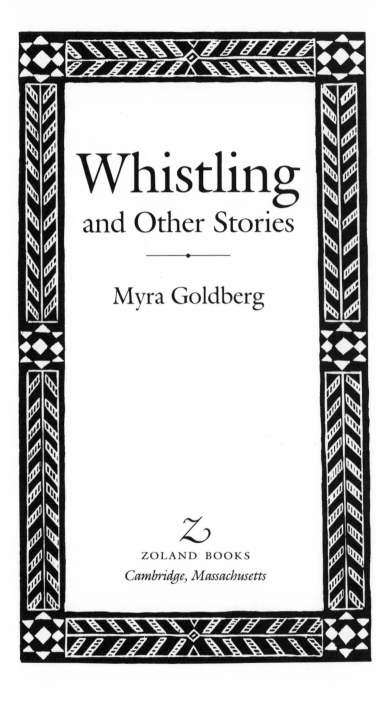

Whistling
and Other Stories

Myra Goldberg

Z
ZOLAND BOOKS
Cambridge, Massachusetts

PUBLISHER'S NOTE:
This book is a work of fiction. Names, characters, places, and
incidents are either the product of the author's imagination or
are used fictitiously. Any resemblance to actual events or locales
or persons, living or dead, is entirely coincidental.

Acknowledgements for previous publication of these stories
appear on a separate page. "Seventh Son" written by Willie
Dixon. © 1955 (renewed) Hoochie Coochie Music (BMI).
Administered by Bug. All rights reserved. Used by permission.
"The Night They Drove Old Dixie Down" by Robbie
Robertson. © 1969 Canaan Music, Inc. All rights controlled
and administered by EMI April Music, Inc. All rights reserved.
International copyright reserved. Used by permission. "You
Never Give Me Your Money" words and music by John
Lennon and Paul McCartney. © 1969 by Northern Songs
Limited. All rights administered by MCA Music Publishing, A
Division of MCA, Inc., New York, under license from ATV
Music. Used by permission. All rights reserved.

FIRST EDITION

Text design by Boskydell Studio
Printed in the United States of America

This book is printed on acid-free paper, and its binding
materials have been chosen for strength and durability.

Library of Congress Cataloging-in-Publication Data

Goldberg, Myra
Whistling and other stories / by Myra Goldberg.—1st ed.
p.   cm.
Contents: Whistling—Issues and answers—Country music—
Emily or How we got here, an American romance—Sylvia and
Wendy —After one—Marrying—Gifts—Story—
Blue spruce—Hair.
ISBN 0-944072-26-7 (acid free paper)
I. Title.
PS3557.03582W5   1993
813'.54—dc20   92-43938   CIP

This book is dedicated to my mother,
Ruth Kronman Goldberg.

———————————

I also want to pay back a little of the
debt I owe to Joanna and Bill Herman,
Martha Collins, Louie Shelleda,
Marvin Resnikoff
and Donald Barthelme,
by thanking them
for their love,
encouragement and support.
As for my nieces,
Devlin and Morgan,
hurrah.

ACKNOWLEDGMENTS

"Whistling" first appeared in *The Transatlantic Review*.

"Issues and Answers" first appeared in *Feminist Studies*. It was reprinted in *Powers of Desire*, ed. Snitow, Stansell and Thompson, Monthly Review Press and Virago Press (Great Britain).

"Country Music" first appeared in *The New England Review*.

"Sylvia and Wendy" first appeared in *The Massachusetts Review*.

"After One" first appeared in *Ploughshares*. It also appeared, translated by Lazare Bitoun, in *Traces* (Paris).

"Gifts" first appeared in *A Shout in the Street*. It was reprinted in *Images of Women in Literature*, ed. Ferguson, Houghton Mifflin. It appeared, translated by Lazare Bitoun, in *L'Arche* (Paris).

"Blue Spruce" first appeared in *Tikkun*.

"Hair" first appeared in *The Kenyon Review*. It was first performed at the Studio Workshop at Sarah Lawrence College and at AC/DC (Washington, D.C.).

The Goldberg Foundation and the Lebensberger Foundation (especially John Mudd) offered moral support and money, the Virginia Center for the Creative Arts and the Millay Colony offered studio space, and Sarah Lawrence College offered a working environment that continues to be respectful and stimulating.

Contents

Whistling

Louie and Laura were on their way to Brooklyn when Laura said: Stop the car. Louie couldn't stop the car, he said. There were too many cars behind them. Besides, why should he stop the car?

Because they hadn't agreed on a restaurant yet and driving without a destination would get them nowhere, said Laura. Nope, said Louie. Driving without a destination would get them to Brooklyn, to that restaurant he'd mentioned, near his wife Iz's apartment, where his son John was waiting to be picked up after supper and taken to Louie's house for the weekend.

How long, asked Laura, to this place, to this restaurant?

Oh, about ten minutes, not counting traffic, Louie said. Laura could tell him a story to pass the time. He liked her stories. He thought she liked telling them to him.

No.

Okay. See if I care. Louie began whistling. Stopped whistling and explained professorially that he had just whistled the first verse of an eleven-minute song in Yiddish that his mother sang to him. It was a song about love, happy and unhappy. He'd forgotten the words, but maybe Laura could remember them.

Laura had never heard the song. But she could make something up, she told him. In English, of course, and about her friend Pru, who was on her mind these days. Only it wouldn't be a song, but a story. Now let's see:

This story takes place in the Catskills. Near Sparta, near where I spent my summers as a child. It was beautiful there. It's still beautiful there, but when I was a child . . .

— Laura, said Louie. I thought you were telling me a love story.

— Right, said Laura. This is a story about Pru and John. And what I meant to say was that Pru met John in the Catskills. And where I wanted to begin was with Pru and me renting a house near Sparta because I'd remembered the place from my childhood — pine trees and berry-picking expeditions and whole days spent rocking in the hammock reading and a million cousins to play with. I thought a summer like that might be good for Pru, who'd been miserable all spring, pale and quiet and hardly eating anything unless I dragged her to a restaurant.

But that's another story. About David, the anthropologist Pru had been living with. He made her get an abortion because he didn't want kids. Then he went back to his wife and had one. A kid, I mean. It was awful.

Louie agreed it was awful.

Our first few weeks in Sparta were awful too. All my relatives were gone, which at first I thought was a blessing, but the town had been turned into a ski resort and we were the only summer people for miles around. All that was left were the pine trees and the berry bushes, so I put up a hammock and Pru went berry picking. Then at night, I read *Uncle Vanya* out loud in the kitchen, while Pru made preserves and we waited for something to happen, anything.

— I spent years like that, said Louie. Waiting.

— One day, said Laura, the hottest day of the summer, a motorcycle drove into the yard and a man in a crash helmet and leather chaps and big stomper boots got off.

— And raped you.

— God no, Louie. He waved to Pru who said she'd met him near the berry patch. She thought he'd moved in next door, but wasn't sure, because she hadn't listened very carefully. He sounded stupid, she added.

I looked over at the man again. He was sitting on the ground, polishing his bike, replacing parts. Periodically, he would start the motor up and Pru would wince and pick a berry from her basket and reject it for spots or mold or missing seeds. Then the man would kill the motor and look over at us and shrug.

Finally we went in to make supper. I set the table, while Pru stared out the window. The man was gone, she said. So was the motorcycle. Maybe we would have some peace and quiet again. I ate supper. Pru picked at a salad. I suggested she bake a pie afterwards and took up *Uncle Vanya* again.

Act one. The doctor enters. He begins to speak about a patient of his who died at Lent. He is conscience stricken. 'I sat down, closed my eyes — just like this — and I started to think. I wondered whether the people who came after us in a hundred years' time, the people for whom we are now blazing a trail — would they remember us and think kindly of us?'

"I've had enough of that play," said Pru. "And enough of this." She gestured toward the pie. "I feel ridiculous. I can't even remember why we came here. I should go back to the city and figure out what I want to do with myself. Go into therapy maybe."

Then she sat down, perfectly still, still pale in spite of the sun over the berry bushes and stared at the star she'd pricked into the pie with a toothpick.

It was a star of David. The black juice oozed out at the points. I had failed. I hadn't done a thing for Pru. And just then — thank God — there was a knock on the door. I went to open it.

A tall man stood on the porch with the moonlight shining around him. "We're neighbors," he said. "I thought you might like some of this."

He lifted up a bottle of white wine. It was all he could find in town, he said, pointing to the motorcycle underneath the pine trees.

I took another look at him. He was slight, with a blond silky beard and wire-rimmed glasses and soft faded blue jeans.

"So you're the guy next door," I said, surprised enough to lead him back into the kitchen where Pru was sitting.

"Oh, it's you," said Pru.

— I knew it, said Louie. I knew that motorcycle man had to be John, at last.

I ran for the corkscrew. John opened the bottle and poured the wine into paper cups. Pru sat motionless, her blond braid crowning her head, her bright blue bathrobe wrapped around her. Then she picked up a knife and cut the pie into pieces. Silence fell. Quite suddenly.

"Why don't you read us some more? Laura was reading," Pru told John, who smiled encouragingly at me.

I read: 'Do stay, I beg you. You must admit you have absolutely nothing whatsoever to do, you have no object in life, nothing to occupy your mind with, so sooner or later, you'll be bound to give way to your feelings — it's inevitable. And it will be better if it happens not in Harkov or somewhere in Kursk, but down here, in the lap of nature. At least it's poetical here . . .'

I looked up. Pru was frowning at me. "I'm a doctor," said John. "I don't get time to do much reading."

— What kind of doctor is he? asked Louie.

— A psychiatrist. Community mental health. John goes out visiting people in their homes in Bedford-Stuyvesant.

— They let him in? said Louie.

— That's what Pru wanted to know. Poor people had pride, she said. What made John so sure they wanted him on their doorsteps.

John traced a circle on the oilcloth with his fingers. Then another. "They need all the help they can get," he said. "We all do."

"Have another piece of pie," I said.

"I'd love one," he said. "I really appreciate this."

He acted appreciative too — seriously considering each mouthful, telling Pru between mouthfuls about his mother, who burned the vegetables and made meat loaf with oatmeal in it and not enough salt.

"I was always hungry," he said. "Except at my grand-mother's farm in the summertime."

Pru leaned forward. "In my family, they counted the string beans so we'd all get the same amount."

They both laughed. I was horrified.

John began telling a story about his grandmother's farm.

I excused myself and started up the stairs to bed. The murmurings continued in the kitchen. I lay in bed listening. John's voice was low and careful. Pru broke in periodically. Then they got quiet. Footsteps started for the door. The screen door slammed. "Shh," said Pru. "We'll wake up Laura."

The next morning a record was playing when I came downstairs. A fire had been lit in the fireplace. Pru was in the kitchen cooking bacon and eggs. John was gone. He's shy, actually, when you get to know him and Pru was embar-rassed because they'd stayed up all night . . .

— Fucking, said Louie.

— Something like that, said Laura.

— Go on, said Louie. What's the matter?

— Where do you want me to go? That's it, isn't it? He rescued her. She didn't have to go into therapy.

— I'm surprised at you, said Louie. Obviously she rescued him. The poor guy. Polishing his bike. Visiting the poor in Brooklyn. Community mental health.

— It's next May, said Laura. Memorial Day weekend. Breakfast time. Pru is out buying groceries. John is in her kitchen ripping up the linoleum. He's reached the floor-boards. Wide. Eighteenth century. The phone rings. John picks it up. Pru walks in with the groceries.

"It's your father." John writes on a notepad. "He wants to know if you'll be down for the weekend. Do you want to speak to him?"

"God no," says Pru. "Tell him I'm not here right now. Tell him I'll take the Metroliner."

"She'll take the Metroliner, sir," says John into the phone. "And she's not here right now."

— Where did you get that dialogue? asked Louie. It's peculiar. What's wrong with them?

— Pru's father is a judge, said Laura. Pru is terrified of him. John is a well brought up person. They talk like that.

— You're making it up, said Louie. The father. The judge.

— I am not. Pru told me. Also, she told John that he couldn't stay at her house anymore. The phone might ring at any moment and —

— That's enough detail, said Louie. We're almost there. Tell me what happened.

— What happened was that Pru went home to Philadelphia for the weekend and John went uptown to his place and a few weeks later, I found a note under my door:

> Join us for a wedding picnic on the
> lawn of the Madison Thorndike
> Memorial Estate in Ossining.
> Saturday, June 30th, 5 P.M.
>
> Pru and John

— It's a research center, said Laura. There was a map on the other side.

— We're here, said Louie. This is the restaurant.

— Two for a booth? asked the manager when they got inside.

Louie passed the breadbasket, but Laura refused it. She wanted to talk about the weekend. She loved staying over at Louie's place, she said, but not with Josh around. Josh got upset. Laura got upset, said Louie. Why make an issue out of everything?

Laura? said Louie, after a while.

What do you want, Louie.

I want to know if your friend Pru finally got married.

Who? Pru? Are you kidding?

I'm perfectly serious, said Louie.

Laura laughed. Where was I?

You were sulking, said Louie. And in the story, you had just gotten the message.

Oh yes. The message. I got the message and went over to Pru's house to congratulate her. A guy I'd never seen before opened the door. He was short and stocky with his sleeves rolled up and the button over here — on the chest — undone. He kissed me. "Pru," he shouted. "It's that friend of yours."

— You married him, said Louie.

— He's already married. He's a family therapist, an old friend of John's. His name is Michael. He was just feeling expansive that day.

— He's always feeling expansive, said Louie. Besides, he knew you. You're a soft touch.

— He knew all of us, said Laura. That's his profession. He sat in the kitchen puffing on a pipe while Pru and John went back and forth about who should marry them — a minister, a judge, a justice of the peace — all out of the question. Then he tapped his pipe against the ashtray. Everyone looked up at him. "How about writing your own ceremony?" he said. "You can get a friend to marry you and go to City Hall afterwards for the legalities."

— This time you objected, said Louie.

— Only to the ceremony, said Laura.

— You didn't like the words they used.

— John wanted to begin with: 'In an effort to secure our mutual growth and satisfaction.' I said it was awful. Pru agreed. John went to sit with Michael. Two hours later, we had a page and a half written out and Clara, from across the hall, promising to play the flute in the background.

— Pru and John asked Michael to deliver the ceremony, said Louie. You felt hurt.

— How did you know?

— That reminds me of Morrison, said Louie. He's chairman of the department. I practically wrote his last article for him. Now he's stuck me with a second section of Contemporary American Problems to teach this summer.

— That's nice, said Laura. We can go to the Catskills when you're finished. You'll have some money.

Louie fingered the oil and vinegar bottles.

— You're giving the money to Iz, said Laura. You've decided to go back to her. Josh needs you.

— Stop jumping to conclusions, said Louie. We were talking about the wedding. We'll talk about this afterwards.

— The wedding, said Laura, was set for a Saturday. On

Wednesday, Pru called me. Something had happened. John had decided that he couldn't go to City Hall. Not after the last marriage. Did I say he was married before?

Well, he was. Just after he got out of the Peace Corps. It was all nonsense, he said, that marriage, but he couldn't make those promises again and take the chance of another divorce.

"What should I do?" asked Pru.

"Gee, that's too bad, Pru," I said.

"But what do you think, Laura?"

"I don't know, Pru. I can see why he's nervous."

— What kind of crap is that? shouted Louie. You knew perfectly well what you thought. You always do. Pru is your friend. You should have told her.

— What could I say? 'Don't marry a man who doesn't want to marry you.' Or, 'Don't marry a man who wants to marry you, but not legally.' How did I know what she should do? Anyway, I was probably right to keep quiet because Pru was deciding to go through with it — the picnic part. "Call, if there's anything you need help with," I said. "Thanks," said Pru. "But I've already made the Greek salad." Then the minute she'd hung up, I called my father.

— Aha, said Louie. Your father enters the scene.

— Don't be silly. He was horrified. He started telling me a long story about some peddler in his village in Poland. Six children from five different women. Phony ceremonies. Rabbis nobody had ever laid eyes on before. "Is she crazy?" he said. "A psychiatrist and a flute player? She agreed to that?"

"This is America, Dad," I said. "It's different here. John was in the Peace Corps. Pru taught kindergarten. They're very ethical people. John's just nervous."

"Who isn't?" asked my father. "The man's no fool. He knows it's not binding. Call her back. Talk to her. Tell her to talk to a lawyer if she won't listen to anybody else."

"I'll tell her," I said. "When she calls back."

Pru never called back. I bought a dress. I got a ride up to Ossining with Michael who assured me there would be appetizers first, so it didn't matter if we were a little late. There were no appetizers. Pru's face was as white as her dress. "Five o'clock," she said, "means five o'clock." Michael rushed to the bottom of the lawn where the young people sat cross-legged in a circle. A flute was playing the Water Music. Michael composed himself. His Indian shirt floated in the breeze. "We are gathered together," he began, "to celebrate this joyous occasion."

I breathed deeply and sat down on a bridge chair with the relatives.

When the ceremony was over, we all signed a petition that Pru brought around saying we were a community of witnesses to the event. "That's not a bad idea," said my father, when I told him. "Maybe the girl's got a head on her shoulders, after all."

— I like the way your father changes his mind, said Louie. He's a good man.

— He likes you too, said Laura. He thinks the world of you, Louie.

Louie beamed. Laura looked across the table. A shining

face beneath a high balding forehead looked back at her. A fringe of soft black hair blew in strands across his head as the electric fan behind him whirled and whirled.

— Louie, said Laura, I think I'll stay over with you and Josh tonight.

Louie was very sorry on the phone afterwards, but Laura didn't see what he had to be sorry for. So she'd taken the F train home. She liked the F train, liked watching it emerge from the tunnel, a mighty *F* blazoned across its forehead in red.

That's enough, Laura, said Louie. You said that you'd stay with me. Then ten minutes later, you were shouting "Stop the car" and running away to the subway.

You left out the part in the car where you reassured me, Louie. Where you said: Josh is used to it. There are women in and out of there all the time.

Did I say that?

Laura looked over at the postcard on the bulletin board.

> Join us. It's beautiful here. Can
> you and Louie make it up for a
> weekend?
>
> Pru and John

Let me come over and comfort you, said Louie.

Comfort me?

I could whistle. You could finish telling me that story. We could make love.

Okay.

Laura? Can I call you back? Josh is about to wake up. I have to take him to the bathroom.

Laura pressed her finger against the black plastic button and laid the phone back into its cradle.

For Christ's sake. You've done it again, Josh. You were supposed to wake up, said Louie.

You were supposed to wake me, Daddy. Josh began to cry. Louie sat down on the Hide-a-Bed beside him. Let me tell you a story, he said.

I'm coming, said Laura on the phone the next morning. I'm coming to the Catskills, Pru, to see you and John again.

"Do you remember David?" asked Pru. She was chewing on a pine needle, watching John who was perched in the rafters of the summer cottage they'd just bought, hammering. "Well, all the time we were living together, his wife kept calling. About the bills and the washing machine. I thought she was crazy, Laura. I pitied her. David had been gone for a year and a half."

"Louie's wife doesn't call," said Laura. "Except about Josh. To make arrangements."

"Lunchtime," called John from the house.

"Okay, John. In a minute. Look, Laura, John says I was an episode in David's marriage, a digression. It happens a lot, he says. To his patients." Pru stood up.

"I'm not hungry," said Laura, walking over to the log where her book sat, the paper still marking her place inside, the pen between the pages. She took the paper out.

Dear Louie,
I never got to finish telling you that story.

Laura looked up from her letter. Pru was walking towards the house. John was climbing down from the rafters.

When we last met, Pru and John had just gotten back from their honeymoon. Pru called me. The honeymoon was fine, she said. Backpacking was fine. Then one day, on the top of Mt. Marcy, John asked her to marry him. Legally, this time. At City Hall. At first, she said yes.

Then she started to think about it, all the way down the mountain, in the car going home, with the radio playing and not a word from John between Schroon Lake and Schenectady and the more she thought about it, the less she liked the idea.

John was right in the first place, she saw, passing Ossining and the wedding grove. It was absurd to rush into things before you knew what you were talking about.

"What are you talking about?" I asked her.

"The marriage laws," said Pru. "I want to know what I'm agreeing to. I've decided to talk to a lawyer. That makes sense, doesn't it?"

"Let me call you back," I said, because just then, there was a whistle underneath my window. It was you, Louie. We were going to see your mother in Brooklyn that night. I was nervous. You had a wife, a child. What would your mother think of me? 'She'll like you, take my word for it,' you said. You were right. Your mother liked me. 'You're a nice girl,' she said. 'They're all nice girls, Louie's friends.'

Laura looked up at the house. Pru and John had disappeared. It was hard to go on with her letter. She folded the paper, slipped it into an envelope, addressed it:

Louie Lichtman
c/o Dept. of History
Brooklyn College
Brooklyn, New York 11238

"The point," wrote Louie, on the term paper in front of him,

is not that the Wobblies were stupid or old-fashioned. They just didn't see, because they were inside the struggle, instead of writing papers about it. Besides, transitional periods are difficult for everyone.

B+

But all periods are transitional, remembered Louie, reconsidering the grade, as the phone rang. No he was not Professor Morrison, Louie told the caller. Professor Morrison was down the hall with the medievalists and what the fuck was wrong with Laura, he thought, hanging up, not a word from her for weeks. For a week, anyway. He dialed her number. Still no answer. Thank God. She might assume something. He picked up the next term paper to grade.

"There's a letter for you," said Professor Morrison, sticking his head in the doorway. "They put it in my box. Somebody doesn't know how to read."

Louie opened up the envelope and read: 'Dear Louie, I never got to finish telling you that story.' 'Good girl,' he wrote in the margin. He read on. Down the mountain, past

Schroon Lake and Schenectady, to Ossining and the wedding grove and Pru telephoning Laura and Laura hanging up the phone. 'It was you, Louie. We were going to see your mother in Brooklyn that night.' Louie sucked his pencil, went back to the beginning. Wrote: 'So Pru wouldn't marry John after all' to the left of the wedding grove. Wrote: 'That makes sense, considering what he'd done to her' next to Pru's decision to consult a lawyer. He stopped. There was a blank on the bottom of the page.

'Good work,' wrote Louie. 'As I said in the margins, everything she did made perfect sense, considering. But was she serious? Is this a joke? The point is,' he scrawled, triumphant, vigorous, 'is this the end?'

No Louie, began the postcard,

> because when I called Pru back the next day, she was already out of town looking for land in the Catskills with John. As for the wedding, they got married sometime between the decision to buy land and the closing of the title or the deed, whatever you call it. They are both scrupulous people and they didn't want to lie on a legal document. Then Pru called one night to find out what procedures you could follow to keep your maiden name intact so I congratulated her and she said, 'Oh well, it seems simpler this way,' and besides, they are going to have a baby.

Louie stared at the postcard. 'The hills around Carthage,' said the printed explanation of the view. 'Laura, in care of Pru and John' had been written underneath. Not an inch of space for a comment had been left. Louie would have to write a letter, but what would he say in it? He rummaged in the desk drawer for a postcard. A Raphael Madonna smiled up at him. Mondrian's view of Broadway lay behind. Then a map of New York State, by Esso. Louie closed the drawer and picked the telephone up.

There was no number, said the operator, in the Carthage, New York, directory for a Dr. and Mrs. John Summerfield or a Ms. Prudence Merryweather or a Pru and John Summerfield-Merryweather.

Check the listings for the next town, said Louie.

Which town do you want? asked the operator. Sparta? Victory Falls?

Forget it. Louie put the telephone down and picked the map out of the drawer.

Several hours later, in Carthage, a real estate salesman directed Louie to the last summer cottage on the road up the mountain. A motorcycle was parked in the front yard. A hammock was swinging from between two ancient pine trees. Louie got out of the car. Anybody home? he called. Nobody answered. Louie walked over to the hammock. There was Laura asleep, a book open on her stomach, the spine rising and falling as she breathed. Louie leaned over. Laura, he said. Laura stirred. Laura, it's me, he said. Laura rubbed her eyes. Louie picked the book off her stomach and closed it. Laura opened her eyes and smiled. It's about time, she said.

Goodbye, said Pru. Goodbye, said John.

Goodbye, said Louie and Laura from the car.

A few yards down the road, Louie and Laura heard shouts

from behind them. Louie stopped the car. Pru ran up with a quart of blackberries and some advice: The Red Herring on Route 9 was a great place to stop if they were looking for a restaurant on their way home.

Laura took the berries through the open window.

Louie started the car again. John told me to take the thruway, he said. What's with Pru?

She's giving us the benefit of her experience, said Laura.

Louie laughed. Then he began whistling. Stopped whistling at the entrance to the thruway to say that Pru and John had inspired him. The words to the eleven-minute love song in Yiddish were coming back.

Sing a minute's worth, said Laura.

Louie shook his head. There's some background material you need to know first, he said. It's a prerequisite to the song.

In English, please, said Laura.

A brilliant young Talmudic scholar and his girlfriend, a beautiful maidele, are parted by circumstances, said Louie.

— What are the circumstances? asked Laura.

— They have a fight. The maidele disappears. The scholar is distraught. Cryptic messages begin arriving at the yeshiva for him. The messages, deciphered, reveal the whereabouts of the maidele. The scholar rushes to the mountaintop where he finds the maidele in a deep sleep and carries her home via the thruway.

— What's the Yiddish for thruway? asked Laura.

— It loses in translation, said Louie. Anyway, there's a test coming up for the scholar and the maidele, so you'll have to be quiet. He pointed to the sign ahead of them: REST STOP

EXIT TO FOOD GAS COMFORT. The scholar is thirsty, said Louie. Before him lies a long journey. Beside him there's an inn. Between the inn and the scholar sits the maidele.

— Can't they find someplace more exciting to stop than a Hot Shoppe? asked Laura.

— Not on the thruway, said Louie. But how will the scholar convince the maidele that he's right before the exit has passed? She doesn't trust him. She doesn't know how much he cares for her.

— How much does he care for her? asked Laura.

— Enough to rush to the mountaintop and back, said Louie.

Laura looked out of the window. We're about to miss the exit, she said. *Click click click* went the directional signal as Louie changed lanes. The scholar and the maidele had passed the test, announced Louie in the Hot Shoppe parking lot. The background material had been covered.

What happened in the song? asked Laura.

Louie unsnapped his seat belt and rubbed the place beneath where the metal had pressed. Then he looked over at Laura. She was sticking hairpins into the mass of curls on top of her head.

I like your hair down better, said Louie.

Laura let her hair down.

A shower of hairpins hit the dashboard.

Louie leaned over and touched her forehead with his lips.

The beginning, he said.

Issues
and
Answers

After the Grubers have left the party, the balding man waves his cigar and opens the discussion.

"Why does Alice stay with Richard?" he says.

"She could do better," says the woman across the table.

Everyone agrees that Alice could do better.

Alice is limited, but likable, the hostess observes.

"Alice is no idiot," says the host. "Richard read her master's thesis last week. He says she writes well."

"My husband is attached to Richard," says the hostess.

The host denies his attachment to Richard. He and Richard went to graduate school together. Now Richard appears on educational television shows. He represents libertarian socialism to the public.

The balding man leans over to me and whispers that the host wants his views taken into account when Richard pontificates.

Everyone hears the whisper. Everyone turns to me. I'm new to the group. I'm cautious. I review the evening with the issue in mind (why does Alice stay with Richard?):

*　*　*

Dinner began with the hostess's announcement that we could sit wherever we pleased. Alice sat beside me. Richard started for the chair beside Alice, but it was taken, so he reached out and tapped the chair on my right, then sat down and looked back over at Alice. He frowned. He shrugged. He opened his hands and trapped a space between them. He peered into the space.

I offered to exchange places with him.

Alice shook her head. "It's good for him."

Three chairs were adjusted, so we wouldn't touch, beneath the table. Three plates of cold noodles and sesame paste were set before us. Alice and I praised the hostess for the noodles. Richard poked his fork among the coils.

"Richard, you ate them on Ninety-sixth Street at that restaurant," said Alice. "You loved them."

Richard reexamined the noodles. "These are different," he said. Then he turned to me.

I inquired about his presence at this gathering, what the connection was. The connection, he said brightening, was the host, an old friend from graduate school, they put out *Participants* together, a theoretical organ. I must have seen it.

I'd never seen it.

The balding man on Richard's right captured his attention by having seen it.

I turned to Alice.

Short, plump Alice with the gray streak in her hair. Alice was pleased to meet me, really pleased, even the corners of her eyes were pleased, even her pocketbook was pleased, she opened it to take my phone number, and I expected a gift, a key chain or a miniature book of verse, merely for being so interesting to Alice.

Alice inquired about my summer vacation.

I told her about my bungalow in the Adirondacks. A screened-in sleeping porch. A washing machine with a wringer outside. A real clothesline strung between the two pine trees for towels and bathing suits. A pile of women's magazines for when it rains. It rains a lot.

"We were thinking of going to Italy next year," said Alice. "But maybe something in the Adirondacks would be cheaper."

"I don't go there because it's cheaper," I said.

"Of course not," said Alice. "How stupid of me."

I shook my head.

The hostess took the noodle plates away. Set the shrimp out. I overheard Richard telling the balding man that forty percent of Richard's students shouldn't be in college. "They're wasting their time," he said. "They don't read. They're completely nonverbal."

Alice began wondering if Richard would like it in the Adirondacks. "He needs people around," she said.

"There are people in the Adirondacks," I said.

Alice looked thoughtful. I became fearful that she'd tap Richard on the shoulder and ask him to consider my description of the women's magazines, the rain, the wringer. "There's no reason for Richard to like it," I said. "It touches me. That's all."

Alice nodded.

Richard told the balding man that his students (the forty percent) would be better off working.

The balding man began listing all the job possibilities for nonverbal people. "Taxi driver. All-purpose kitchen utensil demonstrator in front of Woolworth's."

"Just give me one minute of your time, ladies and gentlemen," I said, leaning over. "Sixty seconds—"

"And I will demonstrate to each and every one of you," said the man. "An extraordinary machine. It chops. It mops. It shops. It picks your socks up off the floor."

"Alice," he said. "Are you really going to eat all those shrimp?"

Alice looked down at her shrimp.

Black beans clung to pink-and-white flesh on the right side of her plate. I looked away and caught a glimpse of the balding man looking puzzled. Then we both watched Alice pass her plate to Richard, who picked the shrimp off with his fork, one at a time, and handed the plate back to Alice.

I began to eat my own shrimp in a rush, for fear that Richard would ask for them, or Alice, for Richard's sake.

"Richard loves shrimp," said Alice.

"So do I."

Chocolate mousse arrived. The balding man grinned and lifted the mousse cup, examined it from all angles. "Pretty," he said, holding the cup out to Alice. "For you."

"Oh no, I couldn't," she said flushing.

"I could," I said, too softly for the man to hear me.

The balding man ate his own mousse, slowly, considering each mouthful.

Coffee was served. Cream and sugar passed around.

ard delivered some observations on the rising cost of raw materials. Quoted himself on the question of underdevelopment. "It's a state of mind," he said.

"Rickets is not a state of mind," said the woman across the table, who'd just had a baby.

Richard stared at her.

"What she means—" said Alice.

"I know what she means," said Richard.

But before he could begin to clarify his own position, the balding man began a story about driving through Georgia.

Everyone waited for the tenant farmer and his rickety children to appear. Instead, the man pulled into the parking lot of a Dunkin' Donuts Shoppe. "I like the waitresses," he explained. "I like their little waists and big thighs. And their beehives. Especially their beehives." He stuck both hands out at the side of his head to indicate a hairdo. "They're the same all over the country," he said. "And I'm the same too. I mean, I always have the same thought."

He paused and leaned forward.

"You have to understand," he said.

He hunched over, wrapped his arms around himself and began rocking back and forth. "That's my mother," he announced, straightening up. "She's about as tall as this table and she wears a wig, a sheitel."

"A beehive wig?" asked the woman across the table.

The man laughed. "So every time I go into one of those places, I get transfixed. 'That woman is a mother,' I think. It always gets to me."

"Alice," whispered Richard. "I'm tired. I want to go home."

"Shh," said Alice.

Everyone heard the *shh*. Everyone turned to the balding man. The man turned to Alice and assured her that he'd lost the gist of his anecdote already.

"Rickets," said Alice softly. "It had something to do with rickets. States of mind."

"You've got a good memory," said the man.

"Alice," said Richard.

Alice shook her head. "Go on," she said. Then she waited for the man to walk into the doughnut shop and discover that this particular waitress was someone he'd known in high school. Gloria Fishel, as a matter of fact.

"I knew Gloria," said the hostess.

"Then you'd know why I stopped going to Dunkin' Donuts after that. Still, I miss the thought. I feel years older without it."

Alice stood up. "I'm terribly sorry," she said. "Richard has to get up early tomorrow morning."

Everyone understood. Everyone had to get up early on Sunday morning sometimes. Everyone said goodbye as the Grubers moved into the hallway to get their coats on. The front door opened, closed again. The balding man moved into Richard's empty seat beside me. Then, when he was sure that the Grubers were outside on Broadway, by the newsstand, checking *The Times* to see that the book review was there, he lit up again, waved his cigar and opened the discussion.

* * *

"Why does Alice stay with Richard?" he says.

"She could do better," says the woman across the table.

Everyone agrees that Alice could do better. The host's attachment to Richard is dismissed. The balding man leans over to me and whispers. Everyone hears the whisper. Everyone turns to me. I'm cautious. I miss my turn to comment, reviewing the evening. I hear the woman across the table say that after she had a baby, Alice called her up to find out what it felt like, being a mother. The woman across the table said she didn't know what it would feel like to Alice. Now Alice is getting books out of the library to help her make a decision. "Can you imagine?"

"Still," says the man beside me, "Richard."

He shakes his head. I go back to the woman-across-the-table's question. Can I imagine? Can I follow Alice and Richard up Broadway, past the drunks, past the men who kiss the air and cry out "mama," past the sleeping doorman, into the elevator cage. A right, a left, a right again, in the corridor upstairs. A key jiggles, a police lock falls open, a light gets switched on inside an entryway.

Light falls on the entryway, on the bookshelves, on Richard's publications and the publications of his friends. Light falls on Alice, checking the mirror, trying to see what she looked like to us tonight.

Alice and Richard enter the bedroom together. Richard tells Alice about the errors he's been noticing in the publications of the man with the cigar. The source of the errors became clear to him tonight, he says. Alice rubs her ankles as Richard decides to denounce the man in his next article. She stares at Richard's guitar in the corner. Then she thinks with satisfaction that Richard never denounces his old friends (bending to pick his socks off the floor, as she leaves for the bathroom).

Wet sounds. Alice returns, breasts encased in a blue woolen bathrobe with a monogram on the pocket. She's been wearing the bathrobe since Barnard. She likes it, just as Richard likes his guitar, his old friends from graduate school. Richard is in bed already, propped up against the pillows, running his fingers down a column of figures in *The Times*.

Alice studies Richard's absorption as Richard studies the price of coffee, replays his part in the underdevelopment discussion. Alice thinks that she has never been as absorbed in anything as Richard is in the financial page. Richard looks up at her. "Aren't you coming to bed?" he says.

Alice takes her bathrobe off and comes to bed. Richard finishes examining the figures, pulls the chain on the lamp, slides down, down, in the bed where Alice is waiting for him, arms wide, nylon and lace in a V between her breasts. Richard rests his head against the V as if he's listening for something. Then he looks up, questioning. Alice nods.

A beer bottle crashes against a lamppost outside.

Alice lifts her breast out of its nylon jacket.

Richard presses his forehead against it, his lips.

He's eager, avid.

Alice is grave, focused. She guides him to her other breast. She rocks him, hands locked around his back.

Richard comes up for air. "Oh Alice," he says.

"Why shouldn't Alice stay with Richard?" I say out loud. "She loves him."

Everyone looks startled.

Everyone looks like they have doubts about me now, although they liked me well enough at the beginning of the evening.

The balding man lights another cigar, a big one, it takes a long time to begin to smoke. "That's a good point," he says finally.

Nobody else says anything.

The hostess suggests a move into the living room.

Everyone stands, except the balding man. Then he stands too. His arm is rising. His fingers form themselves into a fist. He turns to me. He punches me gently, just below the shoulder blade. We grin at each other.

"Hey," says the host. "What's going on over there?"

Country
Music

One of the people in this story is sitting on a broken marble pillar outside an apartment building on the slum end of West Eightieth Street. The other is sitting inside, on her radiator, looking out the window.

It's sunset.

A few minutes earlier, the boy on the pillar had watched the woman walk up the block on her way home from work. She stopped by the renovated brownstones in the middle of the block, waved. The boy looked away. The woman kept walking until she reached him. "Hello," she said, standing by the pillar. " 'Lo," said the boy.

Afterwards, when she's inside, the boy beats his right thigh gently with his palm in three-four time, his left, hard, in two-four. The woman, who is large breasted, long legged, womanish and boyish at the same time, white and living in the same apartment building he does, calls for these measures.

Eight flights up, the woman sits cross-legged on her radiator in a red shawl and dungarees. She's thinking about the boy. He's skinny, black. No, not black exactly, but purplish brown, like a canned plum in heavy syrup, thinks the woman, who's twenty-two, a recent graduate of the Boston Museum School of Fine Arts. His hair is short and his head has a shaved, glistening look. On the back of his neck there's a white spot. Jagged pink edges finger the darkness of his skin.

The sky grows redder, streakier, but the woman doesn't notice because she's thinking about a similar looking eleven-year-old boy she taught to make collages at a settlement house in Roxbury, Massachusetts, last February. The woman was teaching as part of a college work-study program. The boy she taught didn't have a white spot, but he was as skinny and tense as this one and he wrote "fuck you" on his collages. Each time there was a reason. Once, the girl working next to him lifted her silver jewelry hammer and pointed it at his collage. "Hey. That's some fish." It wasn't a fish. Another time, the woman offered to buy his collage — two cattails glued onto a railroad tie. They agreed on a price. The woman went to Soul Food, the record store the boy recommended, and bought two James Brown forty-fives to bring to class. The boy had forgotten the collage at home. He took the records because the woman insisted, but the next week he brought them back. "I can't take no records off you. Somebody wrote dirty words on that thing. My mother made me put it in the garbage." The woman's eyes filled up. She stuffed the records into her shopping bag of collage materials. On her way to her graphics teacher's studio, she lectured herself for feeling so bad. The boy was just a kid. "Fuck you" was just an expression. The shopping bag was getting heavy. She put it down somewhere. She couldn't remember where she'd dropped it the next time she needed it.

If the woman hadn't known the Roxbury boy, she might have invited the boy outside up to her apartment. She might have taken her Craypons, her charcoals, her newsprint pad out of the carton beside the record player and spent a Saturday afternoon on the parquet floor, drawing with him or watching him draw. She might have gone to bat for him at school, bringing his drawings in to show the teacher how good they are, even though his home life is terrible. The woman guesses that the boy's home life is terrible. She doesn't guess that he likes school, is good at music, not drawing, and got suspended for muttering "cunt" at the math teacher, who took away his drumming pad and sticks during a lesson on fractions. As soon as his father, who hates paper pushers, goes to see the principal, the boy will get his pad and sticks returned and his suspension lifted.

The buzzer rings in the kitchen. Nobody answers when the woman says "hello." It isn't the boy buzzing, then running away. It's a big tough thirteen-year-old girl. The girl thinks the woman might have a man in her bed and wants her to get up and answer the buzz. The woman, who stays in the kitchen, hasn't had a man in her bed since her graphics teacher, last February, went back to his wife and two children. She lays her swordfish steak in a frying pan, turns on the flame. The fish sticks.

The tough girl goes outside. She doesn't say "hello" to the boy on the pillar because last week, playing stickball, the boy threw the stick after he missed the ball and hit the girl's little sister in the forehead. The sister was okay, but the girl dragged the boy across the street and banged his head against the iron railing where the garbage cans are chained so he could see how he liked it. The boy said "sorry" three times, but the girl, who still considers him a no-good-soft-in-the-head-pissface won't let him back in the game.

The other boys his age, who have gone in to supper by now, grin and circle an ear with a forefinger when they're asked about the boy. Some boys admire his crazy stunts. Others feel sorry for him, especially if they know his father. Most wish he'd thrown the stick at the tough girl, who is bossier but less important than the big boys shooting lay-ups on the playground at Louis D. Brandeis High School. They double the numbers of circles around their ears to make up for the wish. Nobody likes playing with the boy because who knows what he'll feel like pulling next time?

The boy doesn't know either. Sometimes sitting on the pillar, he feels soft, shapeless, like nothing. If he's got his transistor radio playing by his ear, some of the nothing gets filled and he feels sleepy, but okay. If he's playing stickball, he feels like the bat, until he hits, then he feels like the ball. He runs to get away from the feeling. Right now he's playing the drums he's going to get someday, chrome and ivory plastic, and feels like God or an octopus, all arms and legs. If anybody noticed him, he'd feel sick, ashamed, and play louder, making monkey faces to show how stupid he thinks he is.

A serving spoon bangs against the window gate of the ground-floor apartment. It's the boy's older sister, copper bracelets jangling. She's calling the boy to supper. Supper is late because she's spent the afternoon at her boyfriend's house. The spoon bangs three times to warn the boy that his father, who works nights in a cake factory — sponge cake, ladyfingers, macaroons — has just gotten up on the wrong side of the bed.

The boy starts inside. His father is sitting in a lounge chair with his head bowed, shaking aspirin tablets into his palm. The boy stands, hand on the doorknob. Then he looks up at his sister, grins, slams the door.

Back in May, the boy was sitting on the pillar when a pickup truck pulled into the no parking zone. The woman and two men jumped down. The dark skinny man wearing a ponytail and cowboy boots jogged to the back of the truck, vaulted onto the truck bed, began handing cartons down. A carton marked RECORDS got handed to the woman, who stood below with her arms stretched up. She propped it against the front door. A stocky blond man in overalls carried ART SUPPLIES and POTS AND PANS inside. The woman and the blond man went back and forth to the elevator with a rocking chair, a Dieffenbachia plant, an autoharp, a sheepskin jacket from Afghanistan, a patchwork quilt. The boy found the woman in the elevator trying to fit the plant inside.

"You gonna live here?"

"Not in the elevator, I hope. On the top floor."

"Those two hippies gonna live with you?"

"Those two hippies are going back to Massachusetts." She smiled at him, lifted her long brown hair with both hands, pushed it behind her shoulders.

"Somebody died in there. In your apartment. You better let me go up with you."

"I'd love to. Only look." She pointed to the rocker, the cartons, the instrument case. Her hand jostled the plant. The stem bent. A leaf touched her cheek. "They're supposed to be poisonous." She brushed the leaf away. "If you eat them."

"What if it eats you?"

"Plants don't eat people." The elevator doors began to close. "Hey. How do I work this thing?"

"Press the button." He stepped towards her. She flushed, bent her head, hunted for the OPEN button. The doors closed.

"Fucking bitch." The boy's eyes filled up. He began climbing stairs. Eight flights up to the woman's apartment, then one more flight to the roof. The roof door had a huge rusty hook and eye across it. He lifted the hook, closed the door carefully behind him.

At the roof's edge, he sat down, dangled his legs over the side of the building. From the woman's living-room window, a fire escape enclosed the air around his sneakers. He banged his heels against the brick, found a beat, made his thoughts dance to it: So he'd made it up about the dying. So what! She could have pretended. She could have let him in the elevator cage. He should have walked right in. Snapped the leaf off. Going up. Oh who cared.

"Hello down there." His sister on the sidewalk was walking east towards Columbus Avenue. She didn't hear him. She didn't hear anybody these days, his father said, after he dumped the liver and onions she'd fixed him in the garbage can last night because he didn't eat whore's food. His sister wasn't a whore, but why spend her precious life trying to convince that son of a bitch, she asked the boy who didn't know the answer.

He drew his legs up, hugged them, rocked back and forth. He stood, walked slowly to the chimney where the bottle instrument he'd made was stored. Three Coke bottles, two 7 Ups, a Rheingold, a Schlitz, a Seagram's 7. Graded levels of water rose to make a scale. A 7 Up bottle, half full, came back in his hand to the edge.

He lay on his belly, wiggled until his head, shoulders, chest, waist, were free of the roof. Then he blew the bottle, a soft hollow E. His sister kept walking. He turned the bottle upside down, watched the water spill out, dropped the bottle after it. They met on the sidewalk. His sister looked back. Glass and water in the crack behind her. "Step on a line, break your father's spine," the boy chanted softly. His sister went on walking, east to her boyfriend's house.

When the bottle passed her open window, the woman was at the doorway, kissing the blond man goodbye. A few minutes later, she leaned out, waved as the pickup truck pulled out of the no parking zone. "You'll come visit me," said the man before he left. "I'll have a vegetable garden and we can get stoned and play touch football." "For sure," said the woman. The man was moving to Amherst where he'd do graduate work in American history. Their ponytailed friend was staying in Boston to be near his saxophone teacher. The woman was beginning work on Monday at the Museum of Natural History.

Until a few weeks ago they'd been students, sharing a flat. Every Friday, no matter what had happened during the week, they ate supper together. The woman curried lamb, the blond man baked cranberry bread, the ponytailed man brought Chianti home. A vase of bittersweet the woman had gathered in New Hampshire stood on the table until February when the berries dried up. In April, the ponytailed man began bringing home records that he'd ripped off from the record store he worked in. The woman refused to play them. Ripping off records was an outward visible sign of an inward spiritual state, she said. "It means you're greedy." The ponytailed man said he didn't give a shit if she played the records or hung them on the wall, but he wanted one thing straight: He had different moral standards from the woman, not no morals. "There's only one moral standard," said the woman. "In the sight of God, I mean." "Life," said the ponytailed man, who'd inherited his morals from his father, the Laundromat king of Bayonne, now dead of a heart attack.

He glared at his cowboy boots as if they'd betrayed him, while the woman brooded over the Sunday School sentences she'd found inside her mouth. The blond man, a peacemaker, lifted his bright blue eyes from the rag rug beneath the ponytailed man's boots and the woman's bare feet and inquired gently if the woman's parents might not find their living arrangement as bad as the records. "If they knew."

"If they knew, they'd be wrong, because they'd make the wrong assumptions." The woman meant that nobody in the flat slept with anybody in the flat, according to the rule she'd made. "Anyway, it's my father who'd object. My mother would think this was an adventure."

The blond man, who liked the woman more than he felt

comfortable about, walked to the partly opened window and pushed up, so he could lean out. The woman had a married lover when she'd made the rule, but he didn't feel like mentioning him, because she hadn't, for weeks. When he got back, they discussed whether the real question was their living arrangement versus the ripped off records or the woman's father's view of their arrangement versus the reality or something else altogether. "You two. You're too much for me," said the ponytailed man on his way to the record player. Then the three of them got stoned and listened to Blind Lemon Jefferson, then drove to Cambridge to see *Duck Soup*. After that, the ponytailed man stopped bringing records home and the woman started playing the records they'd already collected.

From the roof, the boy watched the pickup truck move west towards the river. "Those two hippies are going back to Massachusetts." His voice became the woman's when he said the words. He smiled at himself as she'd smiled at him in the elevator cage. "Plants don't eat people," he said aloud pressing his palms against the warm sticky tar paper, raising himself a few inches off the roof. A row of laurel wreaths was etched into the gray stone building across the street. He lowered himself, stood, closed the roof door carefully behind him. Then he ran. Nine flights of circular stairs to the lobby. He was dizzy when he reached the front door. He was humming a Latin song. He'd memorized the words, syllable by syllable, then asked a Spanish kid one day what they were in English. "Your mother. She eats it." The boy had grabbed the kid's knees and brought him down. His mother was not just his mother. She was dead. Now he walked back inside the building to the intercom, pressed the woman's buzzer, positioned his mouth before the circle of holes labeled TALK.

The woman, who was in the kitchen, hanging her frying pan on a Peg-Board hook, laid her ear against LISTEN. "I want to eat your pussy," said a voice from below. She took her finger off the receive button, walked to the living room. "I hate that," she said out loud. The woman's neighborhood in Boston had prepared her for comments on the street. Nothing had prepared her for a voice in her kitchen. Maybe she'd feel safer with gates on the window like they had across the street. She shook her head at the laurel wreaths and went back to the kitchen. The words had risen from the intercom, not climbed in through the window. If she was still doing graphics, she'd make a linoleum block print of her mistake: steel bars, six black words trying to squeeze through, a fiery heaven behind. She'd send it to her friend in Amherst. He'd call to say he loved it. She'd suspect him of being kind, because he was kind, especially to her. Besides, she'd stopped doing graphics in February so she went back to hanging things — a steak knife beside the frying pan, a garlic press beside the knife.

Two weeks later, she followed the superintendent's advice and watched a locksmith install gates across the living-room window with the fire escape outside. "But how do I get out if there's a fire in here?" she asked.

"Same way as everybody else." He pocketed her check, picked up his toolbox, walked through the door she held open for him. "That's no answer." The woman watched the elevator doors close. Then she walked back to their bedroom and looked down, through the remaining gateless window. Eight flights of nothing below.

Beginning on the Monday in May after she moves in, the woman and the boy meet every day. Mornings, the woman is on her way to work at the Museum of Natural History where she paints the dioramas for the stuffed wild animal exhibits. The boy is on the pillar. He's waiting for his father, who's asleep inside, to go see the principal, so he can get back to school before it closes for vacation. The woman says, "Hello. How's it going?" because her father, a Seattle surgeon, used to say that to his neighbors on his way to the hospital. The boy says, "okay."

Evenings, like this June Friday, the woman stops by the renovated brownstones and waves at the boy. She's pleased to see him, because he reminds her that she's got a life outside the museum. Inside the museum, she's worried about the art director's opinion of the grasslands she's retouched for the lion exhibit. The boy looks away into the street. Getting back into the stickball game is more important to him than the woman's friendly wave and the tough girl who rules the game hates the woman. "Hello," says the woman, now standing by the pillar. " 'Lo," says the boy.

Upstairs, on her radiator, the woman sits thinking about the boy, then the Roxbury boy, until her buzzer rings. Nobody answers when she says, "hello." She stays in the kitchen, puts her swordfish steak in the pan. The fish sticks. She goes to the cupboard for oil. The Roxbury boy with the fish collage stands by the open cupboard door. "I can't take no records off you. Somebody wrote dirty words on that thing. My mother made me put it in the garbage."

The woman in the kitchen watches the woman in the settlement house stuff the records into her shopping bag of collage materials. Her eyes fill up. The records sink beneath a sheet of turquoise cellophane. A sprig of bittersweet accompanies them to the bottom. She carries the bag to her graphics teacher's studio, sets it beside his galoshes in the hall wardrobe. "Hello. Anybody home?" Her graphics teacher comes out of the studio. He's wiping his hands on his flannel shirt.

So that's where she left the records. Two hundred miles north of here. In a white-walled studio with a cot, an enamel kitchen table, two stools, a geranium on the windowsill.

The woman carries the vegetable oil bottle to the stove, pours the oil around the fish. The fish sits, surrounded by oil. She pokes the flesh with her fork. Still pink inside. She sits, waiting for the fish to cook, at the kitchen table. Her graphics teacher sits down beside her. He takes her hand, examines it, places it, palm up, on the table. He strokes his Buffalo Bill mustache. His children need him, he says. His son especially.

The woman studies her hand. Ordinarily, she'd be glad to discuss her lover's son, who's wild and wants to be a cop, or a country music singer. She likes taking sane responsible positions, the kind her father used to take when she stood barefoot in the hall, listening to her parents discuss her younger brother. Now, instead of saying, "He needs limits," or

"You've made too much of him," she listens to her lover say, "I've got to go home. There's no way around it." She doesn't say, "What do you mean 'home'?" although last weekend, in New Hampshire, they decided to live together in his studio after she graduates. The deep red blanket she's bought in Filene's for his cot rises before her eyes. She closes them. The color fades. When she opens them again, she's congratulating him on doing the right thing. His children need him, she says. His son especially. He's startled. "I thought you cared for me." She shrugs, walks to the wardrobe, takes her sheepskin jacket out. He begins shouting. It's not his fault. Life is cheap. Art is expensive. "What in God's name are you talking about?" she cries. He doesn't know exactly. He waves at the carved oak wardrobe to indicate that his wife, his children, the woman, his work, have been tumbling inside his head all week like clothes in a dryer. "I'm a serious person," he says. "I should be working seriously."

The woman, who's a serious person too, stares at his face. While she's been looking forward to working in the studio beside him, he's been waiting for her to leave, so he can work. She snaps her sheepskin jacket shut, pulls on her embroidered mittens. "It has nothing to do with you," he says. "I know," she says. "You don't have to say it." On her way downstairs, she counts steps to keep from crying. Then she dashes across the street and begins arguing about the value of the work he's sent her away to do. He's played out. Pathetic. The truth of what she's thinking strikes her like a slap. She covers her mouth with her hand, peers through the iron Common railing at the black wintry tree inside. Its branches are slender, unbearably frail. It's not his work that's clever but pointless, she sees. It's hers. She feels relieved, begins walking again. By the time she reaches her apartment, a seven-mile walk, she's feeling proud. She's forgiven her lover, faced her limitations. She'll move from Boston when she graduates, live alone, get a job. She spends the evening writing job letters: three museums, a nursery school in the slums of Seattle and "would you please send me an application blank for your master's in social work program?" As a child, she refused to go to nursery school. Museums depress her. Her mother is a social worker. Her crayons, her newsprint pad, her etching knife get packed into a carton marked ART SUPPLIES. The world, she tells the ponytailed man, is full of clever people. She's decided to be useful. She doesn't say anything to the blond man, who'd want to debate her decision, until she hears from the Museum of Natural History. Then she hands him the letter. "Isn't it wonderful?" she says.

Her fish has finished cooking. It's white with thick gray-skinned edges. She eats half, crosses her knife and fork on top. "I hate this fish," she says aloud. She walks to the bathroom. Her mouth smiles at itself in the silvery mirror, her eyes swim, her cheeks, enraged, lose their boundaries. Back in the kitchen, she cuts the remaining half of the fish into little pieces, then hesitates. She can throw the pieces into the garbage can or wrap them in tinfoil and put them on the refrigerator shelf.

The door slams downstairs. The boy grins at his sister, who's been late getting supper because she's spent the afternoon at her boyfriend's house. His father looks up. He's in his bathrobe, shaking an aspirin bottle, waiting for the tablets to fall into his palm. He drops the bottle.

Aspirins hide beneath the fringes of the shiny green rug. He bends, as if to pick the bottle up, but pulls off his carpet slipper instead and aims it at the boy. The slipper, a soft brown felt, hits the boy's knee. The boy bends, to rub the knee, which doesn't hurt. "You're like a dog," says his father. "You're under my feet all the time."

When the boy straightens up, he's by the dinner table, holding a steak knife in the air. The knife is cheap steel with serrated edges. It bends when you cut steak. Still, the boy is holding it and his father is sitting a few feet away staring at him. The boy waits for his father to say, "I'll kill you. You'll go where your mother is." His father only stares. His sister's forefinger gets placed beside her nostril to stop the trouble from getting worse. The boy puts the knife back beside the teaspoon at his place setting. He walks across the room, closes the door carefully behind him.

In the hallway he waits for his father to come after him. His father will grab his wrist, twist his arm behind his back. The boy will beg him to drop it. His father will drop it. Both of them will watch the arm swing. His father will leave for the cake factory. Inside, the boy and sister will share a bag of Fritos, sitting on the couch, watch "Police Blotter."

His father stays inside.

The boy listens at the door. No sounds in there. He starts up the stairs, chased by the thought that his father's heart has stopped, like the fat superintendent's did last summer when a junkie cut his key ring off his belt. He stops at the woman's landing so his sister can catch up with him. He whimpers so she'll know how bad he feels. He goes on climbing, when she doesn't appear, lifts the hook from the eye of the roof door, pushes it open, walks across the tar paper to the edge.

He sits, dangling his feet into the woman's fire escape. He feels the weight of his sneakers, kicks. His knees still work. Darkness settles into the sky. He can feel it on his shoulders. He leans forward, looks down. Four men sit on the milk crates below, cards fanned before their chests. Friday night's poker game. A bottle of Jack Daniel's waits by the new superintendent's crate for the winner. A black transistor radio with a long silvery antenna rests on the haunch of a Chevrolet. Latin music.

The boy kicks the brick until he finds the beat he's looking for. His father is still alive. His father isn't some fat superintendent with a key ring on his belt. His father is tall, muscular. Once he was a high jumper. The boy looks at his skinny bare arm. He leans over, licks it. Then he walks to the chimney. He returns to the edge with two bottles. Then two more. Three more. He's on his knees now, a row of bottles before him.

Water follows his breath up the scale. He follows the tune of the transistor below. Softly at first. Then louder. When the song is over, he takes a bow. *"Muchasgracias-señoresyseñoritas,"* he shouts. The announcer announces that the *disco* he's just played can be purchased around the corner, on Amsterdam Avenue. The superintendent looks up. "Hey you. Get off of there."

The boy makes a monkey face, rattles the bars. "Fuck you," he says softly, climbing onto the roof. He kicks his

Coke bottle. The bottle totters, falls, rolls around the fire escape. The card players laugh. The superintendent shakes his fist. The boy jumps down onto the fire escape with a bottle in each hand.

Rheingold gets hurled into the sky. It rolls off the roof of the Chevrolet, shatters at the superintendent's feet. The superintendent looks down. Seagram's lands on a manhole. The superintendent stands. Then he lowers his head, starts inside.

The boy looks around the fire escape. Bars on three sides of him. The woman's window on the fourth. He stares at the window gates. If he stays where he is, the superintendent will jump down and get him. He looks down at his sneakers, then walks to the railing, climbs one leg at a time, over the bars to the next window ledge. He's facing out. There's no fire escape below, only pavement, which tilts, as he looks down, carrying the card players towards him. He turns, faces in, squats, steadies himself by placing his hands on the partly opened window.

Noises at the window awaken her. She's been awakened twice tonight. Latin music. Bottles breaking into a dream she didn't remember. I'm not going to lie here anymore, she thinks, swinging her legs over the edge of the bed, walking naked to the window. His eyes are level with her breasts on the other side of the glass. She looks down at her bare feet. Then up again. His hands begin pushing the window up. She hesitates, reaches up, pushes the window down. Her back is to the pane when the boy disappears. Her hands are pressed against her ears. The boy reappears, face down, on the pavement. Nobody shouts *"Mira"* but the transistor radio gets turned off, the cards get slapped down, the boy gets recognized.

All the way to Amherst, the woman and the blond man listened to the radio. The woman didn't want to talk while the truck was moving. Also, she didn't want to stop anywhere. The radio played oldies. "You never give me your money. You only give me your funny papers." At Amherst, in front of the farmhouse he'd rented, the blond man turned off the ignition. The radio stopped playing. The woman told him that she'd killed a boy. "He was climbing in the window. I slammed it. I stood there falling. No, that can't be true." She covered her ears with her hands.

The blond man stared at the pedals beneath his hiking boots. He leaned across her lap, pulled up the handle, opened the door. "Let's go in." Inside the farmhouse, he cooked hamburgers, while she soaked in a huge tin bathtub with clawed feet. She ate her hamburger in bed, while he sat beside her in the rocker and told her about the summer school class he was teaching. Ambitious freshmen. He was only a teaching assistant, but the students called him "mister" and lied about why their papers were late. A girl with braids on top of her head and granny glasses said his lectures were illuminating. He didn't give lectures. The professor he assisted gave lectures.

The woman began to cry.

Behind her forehead, his hand kept pushing the window up. Her hand kept slamming it. She was prying his fingers from the frame. No. Their hands were locked. No. Sing to me.

He sang "The Erie Canal." He sang "The Riddle Song." Then something from The Band. "And all the bells were ringing. And all the people were singing. La la la la la." His singing voice was thin, plaintive. He wandered from the tune, gripped the lyrics enthusiastically. He knew hundreds of lyrics by heart. The ponytailed man had advised him to forget them. "It'll do your head good." Now remembering, he stopped singing. "I'm not a singer. I'm a graduate student in American history."

"I liked listening. It made me feel like a kid again."

He rocked in the rocker. "Did you know him? The boy?"

"We said hello. How are you. He reminded me of someone."

"I mean. Did you recognize him at the window?" He kept rocking.

"I don't know. I think so. Yes." The woman slid beneath the comforter, stared at the beams above. Then she curled up like a shrimp, faced the wall. The blond man listened to her weep. "Would you like me to hold you?" he said. She nodded. He bent down, unlaced his hiking boots, set them side by side on the rag rug, then climbed, still dressed, into the tent she'd made by lifting one corner of the comforter. He lay propped on his elbow, right hand resting on her forearm. "I think I'm falling asleep," she said.

A naked man was stretched face down between two sawhorses at a country fair. His spine was exposed, extending beneath his buttocks. Somebody handed a fiddle bow to the woman. She tightened the horsehair, drew the bow against the spine.

She woke up startled. Her hand was pressed against her

forehead. Below her, the blond man lay on his back, mouth open, softly snoring. She slid down, so his fingers could find her, kissed his mouth. After they made love, he said, "You." Then they slept again.

It was raining the next night when her taxi pulled into the No Parking zone. Nobody was on the sidewalk. Nobody was in the lobby. The superintendent was in the elevator. He took off his hat when she stepped inside. They stood, side by side, watching the numbers change above the door. At two, the elevator stopped. Then at three. Somebody, the tough girl probably, had pressed all the buttons on her way downstairs. "Those kids. They'll do anything for kicks," said the superintendent. The woman got off because she thought she was about to be congratulated and walked the rest of the way. Inside, her apartment looked strange and familiar, like a distant relative's face. All night she packed. In the morning, she went to buy a newspaper. She circled vacancies. "Hello. I'm inquiring about the apartment you listed."

Now it's fall. Three blocks west, four blocks south, the woman sits in her new apartment looking out the window at the brownstone across the street. Four miniature Doric columns hold up a portico in front. A tree stands to the left, planted by the block association. Skinny black November branches, a few yellow leaves, an iron railing circling around the trunk to keep the dogs away. It's sunset. The woman looks down into her wineglass. She goes to her bookshelf, reaches up.

A newsprint pad comes down in her hand. She bends, places it on the floor, follows it. Her thighs fold to meet her calves. The dirty ridged soles of her rubber sandals face the ceiling. She leans forward. Saturday's sketches pass through the fingers of her right hand. A line becomes a circle, straightens out, frames itself. A second line gets tied into a pretzel. Scribbles make a third pillar thick. Bittersweet sprouts like hair from beneath its flattened top. "Hey. Look at that." At the window again, gates crisscross the view before her.

In a few minutes, the blond man, the woman's lover, will arrive in the pickup truck. He'll jump down, stand still on the pavement, looking at the sky, then start inside. Outside, the red sky will begin to fade. The woman will lose sight of the man as he climbs the three carpeted flights to her apartment. Inside, the doorbell will begin to ring. The woman will answer it. The man will be standing in the hallway. He'll have dope in his pockets, a shopping bag full of vegetables in his arms. Darkness will filter through the window gates, over the woman's shoulder, onto the parquet floor between the two of them. Darkness inside their mouths. "Hello."

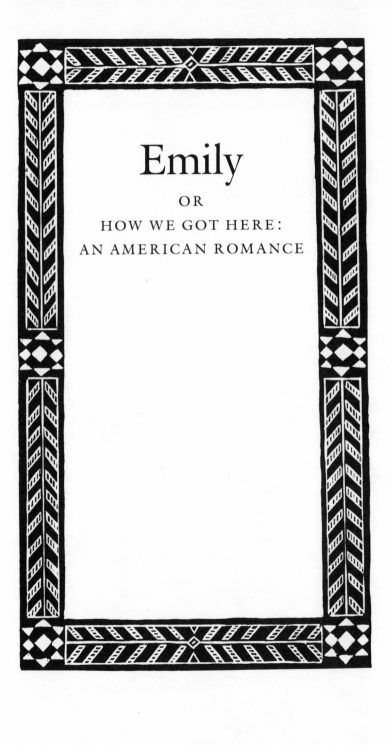

Emily

OR

HOW WE GOT HERE:

AN AMERICAN ROMANCE

Emily came from a town in Massachusetts. But not from one of those Massachusetts towns that make us think: New England. For Emily wasn't from big-city Boston or watery Marblehead or Salem where there were witches. Nor from one of those college towns, whose maples flaming each October by a white-steepled church make people from soot-filled cities nostalgic for other origins. No, Emily's town was a manufacturing town with its maples flaming beside other traditional regional sights: a polluted river with an Indian name, an empty shoe factory with its windows smashed, tenements with wooden balconies on High Street.

And in the worst part of this town, just after the American Revolution, Emily's great-great-great-great-grandfather invented a better cotton loom. Then Emily's great-great-grandfather after the Civil War opened a cotton mill beside the river. Emily's grandfather took the profits from the cotton mill and opened a trust for his descendants during the depression. The trust was permanent, irrevocable, to be used as an income during the lifetime of his grandchildren. Its investments were regional: railroads and shoe factories and bonds for New England's cities and towns to be administered by a bank in Boston.

Years later in New York City, Emily's friend Diane, whose Russian grandfather had peddled pins and pots in Massachusetts, said, "But your family sounds like the kind of people I used to read about. Cool, tall, wealthy, inventive, American Americans living in real American places."

Cool, tall Emily giggled. "You make us sound like frosted drinks instead of people. Well, I guess, we're not unusual where I come from. It's you, Diane, here in this city."

The grandfather who'd opened Emily's trust fund was "a good man" according to Emily's grandmother, who'd been a portrait painter before she'd married in 1910. Still, he was no picnic to live with — silent usually, he had a few responses when his wife tried to speak to him. "You're wrong," which meant the conversation was over. Or, "That seems reasonable," which meant she could do what she'd just mentioned.

When Emily's mother was born in 1913, Emily's grandmother, who'd gotten into bed for the birth, stayed there for the next thirty-five years reading novels and dozing and taking headache powders full of opium. Meanwhile, her husband downstairs turned weirder. For example, during one lonely meal with his desperately serious daughter, he dropped ice cubes down her neck to make her look up at him and maybe giggle.

Upstairs on the hallway walls, the portraits Emily's grandmother had painted before she'd married were hung. Tall cool women in long yellow dresses were seated with fat babies in their laps, with lean men in black suits and stovepipe hats standing beside them. Everyone was drenched in sun-light, but no one had any expression to speak of.

A few months after Emily was born, her mother returned from her own mother's funeral, climbed the stairs and lay down for a nap in the sewing room. Most of the time from then on, she stayed there. So when Emily thought of home, she saw her mother lying in a dark room under a white cotton sheet, and her father downstairs in a worn leather chair drinking martinis. Had things always been like this between her parents? She had no way of knowing. Nor could any of the painted people that she wandered past upstairs and whispered to, tell her anything.

Still, on weekday mornings, Emily's mother got up and cooked oatmeal for them all. And Emily's father, an engi-neer, drove his Chrysler to the airplane factory, where he'd made a small fortune redesigning a plane that once carried bombs to Europe, to carry tourists. And on Sundays, Emily walked between her parents beneath a canopy of trees to a white church in sober dress-up clothes. Then everyone came home to eat roast beef.

The illnesses Emily's mother and grandmother took to their beds were not imaginary exactly, but were compounded of boredom, resentment, underoccupation and the willful re-fusal to cope with lives that had gotten handed out to them like playing cards. So they went on lying in half light beneath the sheets that two generations of Irish women washed and ironed, until their bodies rewarded them with breast cancer.

But despite this gloom, in the world outside, perfection flamed each October in the scarlet maples on the lawn. Purpose flew by in the airplanes Emily's father pointed to as *his* in the sky. And if the sailing trips the family went on rubbed three kinds of unhappiness together causing a conflagration and Emily's mother retired to a bunk below as Emily's father beat his willful daughter into submission with his sneaker or a line, Emily could forget the beatings at will and remember space everywhere in the sea and the sky. Power in her large hands, when her father let her work the sails or take the tiller.

So there were things in that town and in the life Emily led there that were aesthetic, invigorating, and a certain kind of order prevailed, despite despair.

No, the illnesses these women carried to bed were not imaginary. But what Emily, now ingenious enough to design a rigging for her father's sloop, began imagining was that outside Massachusetts — in New York, for example — women did not marry, then take to their beds, but lived lives so rich, various and free that should they ever paint portraits the spirit shining through the painted faces would be bright, eager, angelically intelligent.

So at seventeen, Emily traveled to a college near New York City for girls who were so spirited and rich, it had no rules at all. And she painted huge explosive abstract expressionist canvases and welded sculptures made of broken fenders and stolen traffic signs.

Every evening, she left the campus with a painter in overalls, who had marijuana in the pocket of his fringed doeskin jacket, blond curls to his narrow shoulders and an apartment full of his canvases on Sixth Street and Avenue C.

Emily saw this man standing flat against the Cyclone fence

around the empty lot by his apartment. Looking like the hero of those French movies that were so popular in her college that semester. "The last angel before destruction arrives," she told her roommate, whose father owned a hotel in Las Vegas and who went home without explanation in the middle of the semester. And when this angel took Emily to live with him, she felt safe beneath his wing from something — the painting teacher she'd slept with on the floor of his office and the paintings she might have done, that would have shattered this man and everyone else she cared for.

She took daily walks around her new neighborhood, examining shattered glass and garbage, as if they'd give her clues to her present, future, past. And as the Russian church clock chimed five thirty, which was the hour her father would have started his martinis, she'd wash her hair in a sink full of paint stains, then dry it on the roof.

Twirling and twirling with her hair flying, so that she looked like a Botticelli Venus from the art history seminar she'd liked so much. Turning up the radio in hopes her angel would hear it and climb out the window and onto the roof to see her twirling.

That was Emily in 1961.

Dear Mom and Dad,

I have just smoked a joint in my Lower East Side apartment, which is not, whatever you might think, in an abandoned building. I live here with a painter who considers photography an inferior art form due to its absence of emotion. "Photography is flat, like television," he told me this afternoon. "Whatever places itself between the

eyes and the hand blocks the emotion. The more tech-
nological the medium, the less it has to say." He also
thinks that people with trust funds are living on stolen
money and that I'd do better learning to cook than
doing photography. (I have just bought a camera for
five hundred dollars.) We live very cheaply. We sleep on
a mattress on the floor, but you needn't worry, because
I can't get pregnant. The college says I can come back if
I want to, but I'm learning a hundred times more like
this than by going to college.

Your daughter,
Emily

Emily addressed the envelope of this letter to her father,
who was dry as kindling, but once ignited always acted on his
beliefs, she'd told the angel. Her own belief was that he'd
rescued her from a man she'd begun to feel confused by.
(She'd also felt confused by that painting teacher who'd
turned out to want to sleep with her, when at first she'd
thought he'd really liked her paintings.) For now that she'd
developed all these great photographs of abandoned autos
that looked like animals inside their rusted steel skins, her
angel kept making these weirdo remarks about photography.
Well okay, she'd try what he'd suggested, cooking messes,
until one night she'd burned her hand making vanilla pud-
ding, and with her hand wrapped in a bandage dipped in
olive oil, she'd written that letter to her parents. Then she'd
smoked a joint and decided sitting on the fire escape, as Ray
Charles on the stereo inside announced that he was "The one,
the one, the one you call the Seventh Son," that her life was
too uncertain right now to do anything serious about

photography or anything else. But that she should wait, as she had at school before the angel showed up, to see what might descend upon her doorstep. Then she'd climbed back through the window into the bathtub in the kitchen, washed her hair, ironed it.

Ten days later, Emily's father showed up with a policeman and handed Emily a notice that said he was empowered to take her to a mental hospital. Emily stared at the form's official red seal, then slammed the door in both men's faces. Giggles seized her as they pounded what she'd locked. She climbed out the back window to the fire escape, and ran downstairs to the scruffy backyard. Then west to where the highway blocked the view of the Hudson River. There she settled in a rent-controlled apartment.

Her boyfriend eventually brought over her work shirt and jeans and Hobbes's *Leviathan* (left over from freshman social science) but forgot her expensive Japanese camera. So when she roamed the meat markets on West Street looking at lambs hanging on meat hooks during the day and young men in leather jackets getting into limousines that slowed, but didn't stop, to pick them up at night, she had only her memory to rely on in bed when she tried to light the darkness with what she'd glimpsed.

That was Emily at twenty, whose trust fund checks arrived each month at her post office box because the trust was permanent, irrevocable, no matter how she behaved.

In 1964, Emily stopped taking or making pictures, because she didn't know enough about the world, she felt, to make anything intelligent or even intelligible. Now she wore black turtleneck sweaters and her long dark hair pulled back in a barrette and studied anthropology at the New School. She liked her courses, although she never spoke in class, but what she liked best was sitting on her fire escape in an oversized gray sweatshirt and black tights reading Camus or brochures for the American Civil Liberties Union. These took her breath away. For despite her grandfather's leather-bound American history books at home, Emily had never known that anyone else believed in this: that no one should tyrannize over other people's beliefs. Unlike her father, who thought people who were different from him were inferior and belonged in prisons or mental institutions.

Sometimes after a warm fall afternoon spent reading, say *Walden*, Emily would go uptown to a bar in Harlem and let dark-skinned men with shades and goatees, who looked, she thought, like Thelonious Monk or Malcolm X buy her orange blossoms. Other times she'd return from a trip to some man's apartment, not beaten exactly, but with bruises on her breasts, her ass, or the insides of her thighs. Chuckling, as if she'd won some bet with someone, she'd swear off men altogether and return to the fire escape and *Coming of Age in Samoa*. It doesn't have to be this way, she'd think, spreading her bare knees in cutoffs and examining her large, bare, powerful feet, whose long toes wiggled above the ironwork fire escape. There are other ways to live. But she didn't know for certain what these other ways were or how to find them. She felt those bruises and the men she'd come to hate for manhandling her had paid her back for something — her perverse insistence on going on and on until she'd found one.

* * *

Emily was twenty-seven in April 1968. Working on a master's thesis in the reference room of the Columbia library, with the sun pouring in from the skylight on the thesis she'd decided to do perfectly to redeem the years she'd spent avoiding it.

"The evidence suggests," she was writing as a tall skinny man with shoulder-length curls leaned over her shoulder to read what she had written.

"Join us," he murmured when he was done reading.

How intimate the gesture, she felt. Still, she covered the manuscript with her hand as he said in a politely earnest voice, "We're on strike. We're shutting this place down. I think you'd better leave with me."

She left with him. Indeed, she preceded him down the winding marble staircase, then stood outside on the library steps blinking in the sun, as crimson banners got thrown over windowsills and her Botticelli hair blew this way and that in the wind.

"We hold these truths to be self-evident. That what makes us sick at heart inside these classrooms is the same brand of murderous bullshit that napalms children in South Vietnam and builds chain-link fences to keep black people out of their own neighborhoods. And ain't none of us gonna renege on this commitment: to hold this place for ransom until it returns to what its commitments should have been all along: democratic education and research directed at supporting the liberation of the world instead of its destruction and enslavement."

The man who spoke wore a velvet smoking jacket, but lacked the curls of the man beside her. Who looked, Emily whispered as they lay side by side in sleeping bags on the stone floor of the math building, like a Cavalier poet. Other people, looking at Emily that night, saw someone almost six feet tall, silent, beautiful, with an Indian maiden's face and hair as black and shiny as a lake upstate after a rain. Powerful, they thought. A presence.

After the strike, Emily and the cavalier had a very nice affair until it turned out that his real girlfriend was pregnant so he married her and said goodbye to Emily. "That's cool," she said, wondering why when she spoke to men, she was invariably lying.

"I've lived in a dream. I can't understand how I got to be thirty," Emily told the silent analyst from the couch she was pretending was a raft, as she floated three times a week down a river that was the story of her early childhood. Above her pillowed head were puffy clouds that were the analyst's interpretations. Sometimes tears rained down her cheeks as she talked about how boyfriends who'd seemed so kind and gentle at first turned out to be shitheads and even beat her and how she'd lived in the same rent-controlled apartment for twelve years and tutored sixth-graders once and got a master's degree in a field she didn't care for and that was it — her life. Without real work or a spiritual life or even the commitments that her miserable parents had made to each other.

After her sessions, she'd feel crumpled, like her tissue, but her life changed not at all. Still, she saw the silent analyst every other morning and there was some structure to her days and someone to talk to in a world where everyone else had gone to work or gotten married. One day a telegram came that said her mother had died and after swearing to her analyst that she'd stand up to her father, which was like a pledge to God, since the analyst, like Him was so distant and so far away, she drove her BMW up the turnpike to Massachusetts for the funeral.

"I want you to know," she began as she walked home beside her father between the Concord grapevines, now loaded with October's purple and slippery pleasures. For she was prepared to tell her father that she held him, in part, responsible for her mother's misery, but then her heart started pounding at the thought of actually speaking the truth to him. "How important you were in my mother's life and death," she murmured.

"Your mother never much cared for me, sweetheart," he said opening their door.

In the house, with his drink in front of the television set, her father nodded his permission for her to take her grandma's portraits and the quilts from her mother's bed back to the city. So Emily loaded up her trunk and shook hands with him before she drove off.

Everything went into her closet until she figured out what to do with these things. Meanwhile, her check to her analyst bounced and he'd refused to see her until she wrote him a replacement, which she refused to do, because he'd been such a distant shit. Then she took the opportunity to leave someone who'd done nada for her in the five years she'd been seeing him.

✳　✳　✳

"In Worcester, a man went to a well that had been dry for many years. Finding the bucket full of water one day, he dropped it and never returned. Was this surprise? Or something else?"

In 1972, a Christian practitioner who spoke in parables replaced the analyst who had failed her in 1970. For Emily had begun painting oil portraits of individuals who looked like Puritan judges in Barcaloungers with Indian maidens sitting beneath them cross-legged on the floor in blown-up photographs of New York City apartments. Around the photographs like frames, she'd cross-stitched rivers, valleys, mills and towns.

She'd gone to the practitioner, because after her first art show she'd stopped painting. First because her painting teacher from college, now an extremely famous man, had come to see her show. "I expect great things of you," he'd said, then invited her to his apartment for a drink, which she refused. For several weeks after that she'd sat in her apartment with moldy dishes in the sink, worrying that she'd ruined her career by not offering to sleep with him and fearful that she'd have disappointed some long line of women if she had. Meanwhile, her paintings, she felt, would enrage some line of men, looking blankly or critically at what she'd hung up.

This feeling had some basis in the reviews her show was lucky enough to get: "Exquisitely crafted, the focus on medium here leaches energy from the content." And: "It's hard to know why this clever and original young woman has worked so hard to put these trivial items together."

She'd started worrying, she told the practitioner, that she would never have a child and took to reading Darwin every afternoon because she felt *On the Origin of Species* had something to do with her dilemma.

Finally, with the man's help, she began sketching again, mothers and children in Abingdon Square Park while she sat waiting for her friend Diane, whom she'd met at Columbia during the 1968 strike.

"It's possible that I never had any idea how to make friends. Only in graduate school it didn't matter, because there were always people, especially men around," she'd told Diane over tea at Patisserie Lanciani. Stirring and stirring, she gazed into her cup, as if she'd find some answer at the bottom. "Not that it ever occurred to me that men could be my friends." She raised her head and looked directly at Diane's blue eyes. "Or that I should even like them before we slept together."

Diane's next visit took place in Emily's apartment. For Emily was in bed, because her back had gone out after her practitioner was diagnosed as having lung cancer. "My orthopedist suggested that I take it easy," she said by way of explanation. But six months later, as January and 1980 approached, her back was no better and her feet had gotten bad because she'd stopped using them, and Emily, newly graying, was using a wheelchair, which had to be lifted by her Haitian driver into her BMW, so she could get to her new psychotherapist, a woman. At home, she studied economics by reading a text flashed onto her ceiling with a Korean business student beside her bed, so she could check on what was happening with her money, which seemed to be diminishing.

* * *

"My back has convinced me that I can't support a revolution," Emily told Diane on her next visit. "Because I'll always need expensive shoes and especially good mattresses. Also, my doctor's bills are enormous."

Meanwhile she hired a lawyer to check on her trust fund, which her father, who'd laughed at her wanting to know about her finances, had given to someone he'd met sailing to manage. The man took the money from railroads and municipalities and put it into oil in Colorado and real estate in Phoenix. The Korean business student, who was the only person Emily saw regularly besides her West Indian housekeeper, began looking like an angel to her as he sat murmuring by her bedside about takeovers and junk bonds and how to hold on to the income she was dependent on.

"Help," she shouted one night, when she woke up sweating. For she'd gotten it: that she was alone and lonely and childless and skill-less and getting older and getting older. But what she didn't get was how all this had happened to her, Emily.

The next time Diane visited, Emily looked down at her fingernails, then raised her head from her wheelchair and said, "I feel I ought to tell you, dear, after all we went through at Columbia together and all those talks we've had — about my family, and women, and the war in Vietnam, that I've decided that President Reagan has been doing a wonderful job. Because why should people who take care of themselves take care of people on welfare who keep having kids, when everyone knows they'll only turn out to be muggers and dope addicts?" She poured some tea from her grandmother's teapot into two exquisite Japanese cups and handed one to Diane.

"But who in this country takes care of themselves? Not the corporations certainly, or the wealthy." Diane was wrinkling her nose as if the room had begun to smell of something. Noticing the cup her friend had handed her from her wheelchair she murmured, "Lovely."

"Furthermore," said Emily, "I've finally realized that the Russians understand force and that's all — like my father. So the only way to keep our liberties intact is to threaten them with whatever we've got, including nuclear weapons and to use them if we need to." She was gazing at her long fingers, which she spread. A long time passed in silence. Emily made two fists and dropped them into her lap and lowered her head as if waiting for something.

Well, what can you expect from a rich person? thought Diane during the silence. And she's not even Jewish. Or Italian. She said, "What liberties? If everyone is dead." Angry that this friend who'd been so eager and brave and determined to escape the narrowness of the world she'd been born into should be too crazy to understand that when you kill people they stay dead. Tears came to her eyes. Because Emily, who seemed simultaneously like a cloistered Victorian lady and her own rebellious teenage son, had been lying in this darkened room coming to crackpot conclusions about a world she'd hardly ever lived in. Still, when the subject turned to Tolstoy, whom Emily said her new therapist knew for certain was narcissistic and probably even schizophrenic,

Diane stood up and went home, for there were some things, she felt, that shouldn't be handled by simplistic sloganeering, psychological or political.

Americans, she decided on her way up Hudson Street, were wonderful at building things and admirable about the space they gave each other, unlike her relatives who spent their lives pushing and shoving each other, but they had no ear for ideas. And no idea how their own country worked or got run.

This is how Emily at forty-two, now that her only friend had left her, thought about herself: "I'm problematic," she told her therapist. That is, she knew she would never have a child (which made her weep). As for the rest — her life — her work, well, sometimes she wasn't sure she could untangle all her problems. Sometimes when she wasn't feeling defeated, she thought she could. At other times, she wished that her grandfather had never opened up her trust fund. For her money had not only isolated her but had created the illusion, since it could buy time in the form of servants and gadgets and even hours of understanding from a therapist, that it could stop time and keep Emily, who was not a gadget, from wearing out before she found the solution to her character, her history or her problems. Still, on days she felt especially despondent about solutions, she felt especially exalted by the clarity with which she saw — over maples and airplanes, civil liberties brochures and striking students, mothers lost to martyrdom and fathers lost in bottles — that if any of it had been different, all of it would have been different and so, of course, would she have been.

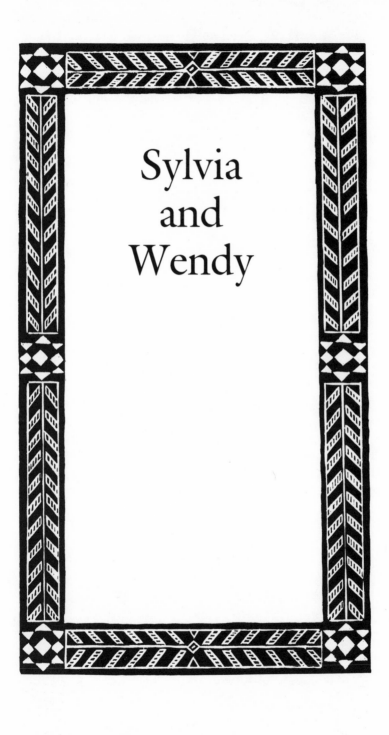

Sylvia
and
Wendy

"Do you think they put us together because we rhyme?" asked Sylvia Fein.

"No," said Wendy Klein. "It's because of the pocketbook store."

Sylvia stared at Wendy. Wendy didn't look puzzled or irritated by her question. Relief flooded her.

"I forgot," said Wendy. "You're not from the city. The store is orthodox. Run by real Jews, I mean. Not like us. I bet the dean checks out the pocketbooks at Bloomingdale's, then goes to Fein and Klein downtown and picks one up for half. We commemorate her last purchase. Something structured. In alligator. With a big gold clasp."

Sylvia nodded, although she had no idea what a structured bag might be and her own imaginary dean was a silent, meditative woman, so sick of questioning herself (should both girls smoke? listen to folk music?) that when a Fein appeared near Klein on her freshman housing list, she heard a click and made them roommates.

Wendy squatted, reached into an open cardboard box,

lifted out a sculpture. A rough clay woman got set on the floor, arms outstretched, legs spread apart.

"Did you make that?" Sylvia could hear the awe in her voice.

"It's an old thing. I did it my junior year."

"It's wonderful."

"That's interesting. That you like it. Most people find it crude." Wendy reached into the box again. "This is Tibetan." She lifted out a small bronze horse. "Or Greek or something. My boyfriend Jonah gave it to me. He's thirty-seven. When my father found out about him, he threatened to press charges. So now I just don't tell my parents anything." Wendy smiled, opening her blue eyes wide. "I'm sixteen. I was in the rapid advance class in junior high. Jonah would be charged with statutory rape." She brushed her crinkly blond hair behind her shoulders. "Aren't you glad to be away from your parents?"

Was she glad? Sylvia wound a curl around her index finger. Did she have parents, in the usual sense? Had she been away from Corinth for long enough to know? Would she be away forever? Was this the beginning of forever? The curl tightened until her flesh began to hurt. Something wonderful would happen if she could only stop questioning herself and start speaking. "I don't have parents. Just my father and Uncle Jack."

"Who's Jack?"

"My mother's brother. My father is crazy about him." She looked at Wendy. "But the only time he says anything is when Jack does something wrong."

Wendy nodded knowingly.

"They run a clothing store together. 'Jack,' says my father. 'You shouldn't make that boy lift those boxes. He'll get a hernia. Life is hard enough without a hernia.'" She frowned at her desk.

"What does Jack say when he gets yelled at?"

"Something like — let me think — 'I'm getting agitated. A few more episodes like this and I'll be forced to walk out.' He did once. After my mother died. She died suddenly. Of a heart attack." Sylvia stopped, trying to remember what the subject had been.

"Jack left after that."

Sylvia nodded. "My father closed the store as if Jack had died too and sat reading the letters of Justice Oliver Wendell Holmes for a week. 'Every argument has an inarticulate major premise,' he said when Jack got back. My father talks like that. He tries to summarize a week's worth of thinking in a sentence."

"Now let's see." Wendy's hand covered her eyes. "Who do they remind me of?" She took her hand away. "It's the guys who run the United Cigar on Ninety-first Street," she said triumphantly. "One is incredibly pale with no — I mean no — hair. He's the hopeless intellectual type. The other is fat and chatty. I think he's got a heart condition." Wendy frowned at her desk. "They sell *Women's Wear Daily* and The *Psychoanalytic Review*." Wendy coiled her hair, opened a bobby pin between her teeth, fastened the coil on top of her head. "Come on. This will be the counter." She walked to her desk, shoved it against Sylvia's. "You'll be your father. I'll be Uncle Jack."

Sylvia started towards the counter. Paradise before her.

The games she'd played inside her loneliness spread, like merchandise, on the surface of their maple desks. Wendy's blue eyes inviting her, promising her. She bumped the desk leg. "Jack. The flannel shirts have come in. Feel that." She rubbed thumb and forefinger together. "One wash and they'll be shredded." Tears in her eyes. "It's a terrible thing, Jack. Decent, hardworking people come in. They expect what they get to last forever." She looked at Wendy.

Wendy shrugged. "Nothing lasts forever."

"Maybe I should call the manufacturer."

"Go ahead. He'll tell you, 'Life is hard. Things are rough all over. You want flannel shirts that last?' " Wendy pounded her chest. " 'Make them out of nylon.' "

Sylvia laughed. Wendy laughed. A tall girl in a grown-up lady's bathrobe appeared at the door. "Man, that's rudeness. I've got a thesis to write."

"I'm terribly sorry," said Sylvia.

The girl went away.

"I'm terribly sorry," said Wendy in a voice so ashamed that Sylvia said, "Hey. You can't play me."

Wendy knelt by her suitcase.

She'd explain, if Wendy ever spoke to her again, that she hadn't intended to imply that Wendy (who looked like Ingrid Bergman only plumper) would want to play her. (What serious person had bangs above a pale moon face? What pretty person had jiggly white thighs and baby fat breasts?)

Wendy stood up. A long flesh-colored nightgown dangled from her large hand.

"How beautiful," said Sylvia.

"It's Crayola colored." Wendy held the gown against her chest.

Sylvia nodded. She knew about Crayolas.

The sun was shining. The sun was shining loud, like cymbals, on their pushed-together maple desks. Sylvia stretched, trying to remember the name of the feeling inside her. Feeling empty. Feeling full. Feeling there was nothing she wanted but to lie there, looking at the sun on the surface that had turned into a counter piled high with flannel shirts last night.

"I'm not used to getting up so early," said a voice from the other bed. "You'll have to wake me."

Sylvia went to stand by Wendy's bed. "Get up. It's morning." She looked at Wendy's broad shoulders beneath her nylon nightgown straps.

"Aw, Ma. Get off my back." Wendy sat up, pushed down her blanket, stared at her ankles. "You're the only friend I've got who has American legs. Thin calves, I mean. Except for Carol. The one who ran away to Phoenix with her English teacher." She looked at Sylvia.

Sylvia was a friend. Wendy had accepted her.

She learned to talk again. Listening, at first, to Wendy. The light from the window was "like Vermeer." Katherine, across the hall, was "horsy, asexual." Sylvia's sweatshirt had "the texture of my grandmother's upper arm."

One day Sylvia brought her own observation back from philosophy class. "Every time the girl next to me opens her mouth, I think she's going to kill something."

"What does she murder?" Wendy leaned forward. "Feeling? Atmosphere?"

"She doesn't murder anything. She just stops things." But Wendy was still leaning towards her, so Sylvia went on. "She reads the simplest sentence in the book aloud, then asks the teacher to explain its meaning."

Wendy nodded knowingly. "She reminds you that you're in a classroom."

Sylvia tried nodding knowingly, a few days later, when Wendy returned from music class. "The professor is like Ray Charles," Wendy said. "Only white and not blind."

"You mean he shouts?"

"I mean he puts out."

And when Wendy didn't mind her being wrong, she tried comparing them. "My neatness comes from fear. Your messiness from generosity."

"But I like it that you're neat," said Wendy.

She went further, a few weeks later, offering her help with Wendy's William James report because Wendy said she'd never thought about abstractions.

"You're so good at that stuff," said Wendy, "that if I let you help, I'll never learn how."

Sylvia left for the library.

Wendy was in her nightgown when she got back. Two Mounds bars, a container of milky coffee and *The Varieties of Religious Experience* sat on the desk before her.

"My dear," said Sylvia. "You're not going to believe a word of this."

The line came from Wendy's favorite game: "My Aunt Rose and Uncle Max in Sarasota."

"Shoot, sweetheart." Wendy's bare feet went up on the desk.

"Wait. This is real. Some guy wanted directions to the reserve book room. When I told him, he grabbed my arm. 'You must find it frustrating going to a girls' school,' he said."

"That game is called 'Date.'" Wendy's feet came down. "Now would you please look at what I'm doing?"

Sylvia had a friend. She had a best friend. Someone to characterize: "You seem impulsive, but you're cautious, in fact." Someone to trade things with (her sweatshirt for Wendy's flesh-colored nightgown; the B minus on her poem — "Your prosody is rigid; your diction abstract" — for the C on Wendy's economics paper — "You're writing, it seems, from some stream of consciousness." Someone to sit beside at breakfast when Katherine began the story of her trip to the housing office to complain about her roommate. And when Katherine reached the part where the dean assured her "a variety of criteria" had been used to match them, Sylvia leaned forward as Wendy asked, "What criteria do you think she was talking about?"

"Do you smoke?" said Sylvia. "Do you listen to folk music?"

Wendy laughed. Sylvia laughed. Katherine laughed.

"Katherine hates life," said Wendy afterwards.

How could Katherine, with her loud laugh and her Russian crossword puzzles, hate life? reflected Sylvia on the library steps. Wendy must see depths. She saw only surfaces.

A few weeks later, feeling nervous before her appointment with Financial Aid, Sylvia suggested the game "Dean" to

Wendy as a way of preparing. Wendy could be dean. Sylvia would be Sylvia.

"How do you feel, Sylvia?" Wendy lifted her Magic Marker from the desk. "About the progress you've made this term?"

"I have no idea. I didn't know I'd made any."

"No idea," Wendy pretended to write. "Doesn't know she's made any. Give the girl two hundred dollars."

"Please, Dr. Dundee. Could you make it four hundred?"

"I'm shocked at your greediness. Three hundred and fifty and that's final."

The real dean, a pale young graduate, wearing black eyeliner and a red plaid kilt, glanced at her file, then smiled. "You're doing exceptionally well, your professors say. How about taking it a little easier?"

She felt shocked. Her prosody was rigid. Her diction abstract. How could she take it easier? And why work to take it easier, she wondered on her way back to Dewey House, unless the dean removed the file that said how serious she'd been at first.

But Sylvia forced herself, a few days later, to stop listening to her philosophy professor and to look at her instead. "She holds her hand inside her blouse as if her heart hurt." She slipped her hand inside her polo shirt to show Wendy, massaged the breast, took her hand out. "She was in love once, I've decided. With a student in Heidelberg. He got taken to a concentration camp. She wants to make sure he's still alive in there."

"Oh come on. She's feeling herself up."

"In class?" Sylvia felt shocked.

Wendy picked up *ARTnews* and began leafing through.

"I've got it," said Sylvia.

"Got what?"

"The difference between us. Your woman's hand and breast are real, but her lover is imaginary. My woman's lover is real, but her hand and breast — it's the past she's feeling, not the flesh exactly." She looked at Wendy.

"I'm going to the snack bar. These discussions are making me thirsty."

Wendy returned an hour later with a Coke.

Sylvia was so relieved to see her, she said, "You know, I've been thinking about what you said and now it makes sense to me."

"We're very different," said Wendy.

Sylvia got into bed, pushed down her blanket, stared at her legs. There was no point in feeling sorry for Wendy's boyfriend Jonah, she decided. Just because Jonah (who looked more like her father than the Albert Camus she'd imagined) idolized a girl who seemed contemptuous of him.

"Wendy's a Rhine maiden," Jonah had said before they'd left for a motel.

Wendy had glared at him. "Does everything have to come from books?"

Wendy was too different for her to judge.

We're very different, Wendy had said.

Sylvia pulled up her blanket and saw a layer of sameness in their sentences that, like the pastry in a napoleon, kept the layers of difference together and apart. "What kind of napoleon?" she made the Wendy in her mind inquire. "The kind my mother brings home from bridge because 'it's a crime to throw such beautiful food away.' Or the kind my friend Larry gets from the Puerto Rican bakery. Eating one is like shooting up, he says. The sweetness gives you a jolt, even if the filling tastes like kindergarten paste." Sylvia put her head on the pillow. She might be too different to judge Wendy, but she could imitate her, make her talk inside her head.

"I didn't think," she wrote her father at Thanksgiving, "that you and Uncle Jack would mind my spending the last part of Christmas vacation at Katherine's."

"Sylvia," said Katherine. "This is my brother Jake."

He was blurry, in motion, flipping the dial on the radio as she and Katherine climbed into the car.

"You're playing a radio tune," she said.

"There's a system behind my apparently random selection." Jake looked respectfully at her. "But I didn't expect anyone to notice."

"Sylvia notices everything," said Katherine. "Why else do you think I'd bring her home?"

She felt embarrassed, between them. She looked away as Jake took his sneaker off the brake and wondered if what Katherine had said about her noticing was true. Because the one thing she'd never noticed — apart from how baggy her tights had become — was that she had characteristics, like other people had, for other people to notice.

* * *

Jake was different from her, listening seriously as she pointed out that the leafless maple they were walking towards held a revelation, but that you had to comprehend — all at once — the place where the trunk split and the shape the branches made against the sky, to see it.

Then she listened seriously, as he explained their difference: his tree was revealed through information (there were growth rings inside) or action (he'd climbed it), but looking at things, the way she did, only confused him.

He looked at her. He brushed his crinkly blond hair from his pale forehead. "But you already know that. I'm invariably telling people things they know already. Or things they're not interested in."

"No." she said.

He kissed the top of her head. "You'll have to come to Cambridge. My room is odd. It looks rectangular, but it's asymmetrical, in fact." He knelt, picked up a stick, drew a soft right angle in the pine-needled earth. "See, I have the corner room." While she looked: at the stick, at his throwing arm, at the red wool scarf dangling from the neck of his navy blue pea jacket.

"See you," said Jake, when he dropped her, three days later, in front of Dewey House. She stood, wondering what "see you" meant, then carried her suitcase back to her room.

Wendy sat on the bed, her long hair cut into curls.

"Oh hi," said Sylvia. "How was your vacation?"

"It was okay. Jonah went to Greece. And I went to Bloomingdale's for a haircut. A photographer in Cruisewear bought me lunch. I slept with him." Wendy crossed her legs.

"Jonah took advantage of me. He must have known how bad he was in bed. That I was too inexperienced to know the difference." She looked at Sylvia. "How do you like my haircut?"

All the way to Cambridge, Sylvia practiced, hoping her sentence would sound lifelike when she reached Jake. "Hello. It's me. I came to see your room."

"Come on in." Jake stood at the door in polo shirt pajamas with the neck bitten out of shape. He'd been fluish, feverish, that was why he hadn't called, he said.

He picked his sweatshirt and the Garrard catalog off a torn leather chair, handed her a teacup full of whiskey.

Sylvia sat on the bed. "As a matter of fact, I didn't come to see your room. I came to see why you said 'see you' then didn't call." She stood, toured the room. "It's not asymmetrical, exactly. It's closer to whatever it's called when slanty lines run parallel" — poured more whiskey into her cup — "if you don't mind," and climbed back on the bed.

He wondered from the chair if all the versions of her "seeing" sentence were really one sentence, like the paper tree he'd constructed in linguistics.

"I came to see you," she said, as he climbed onto the bed, "because I felt like it."

"You sat on the bed. Talking about Wittgenstein," said Wendy.

" 'The world is all that is the case.' And we ate cream cheese and pumpernickel. It was wonderful. Then we went to bed. Only we didn't — sleep together — until morning.

I'm not sure he knew how." Sylvia stopped. "He's the smart-
est man I ever met."

"I would have been furious," said Wendy.

Sylvia's eyes filled up. She felt sorry she'd told Wendy. She
watched Wendy walk to the window.

"I've got a new game," said Wendy softly. "I made it up
while you were gone."

"Shoot, sweetheart."

"It's called The Future." Wendy covered her eyes with her
hand. "Bloomingdale's. Ten years from now. The pocketbook counter. You teach philosophy and have three kids.
I'm a sculptor. The first line goes: 'Wendy! Sylvia! I'd know
you anywhere!'" She uncovered her eyes and turned
around.

"Wendy! I'd know you anywhere."

"No, you wouldn't," said Wendy.

"Wendy's at her studio a lot. I'm usually asleep when she gets
in. And even if I weren't" — Sylvia pushed Jake's hand from
her breast — "she doesn't waste time talking anymore. I
mean it." She shook her head over the mystery, the changes
that Wendy had gone through in the last eight months. The
skinny, silent, hardworking sophomore who had appeared
to take the place of the chatty, plump, playful freshman.

"I don't believe in talking *personally,* you know? It's boring" was Wendy's last pronouncement on the subject.

Still, they were still roommates, though Wendy was rarely
home.

It was February now. Snowy. A snowy, lonely Sunday,
the kind that made Sylvia feel irritated, blue. Because in an

hour, she'd get on the bus and Jake would disappear and to keep herself from disappearing too, she'd think, I'm a sophomore. I should have worked. I bet Wendy was working all weekend.

Last Sunday afternoon, it had been lonely in their empty room when Sylvia came back from Cambridge. So she'd wandered to the snack bar where Wendy had been sitting, staring into her coffee cup. "Oh hi," Wendy had said listlessly. "How was your weekend, eh?"

"Okay." Sylvia slipped in beside her. "Well, at least we saw a movie." Then, having played down the fun they'd had, because maybe, oh maybe, Wendy didn't want her having fun with someone else, she'd slipped into last year's game and giggled. "Jake loved Belmondo. But I prefer your Uncle Max, the taxi driver in Sarasota, remember him? Ha ha ha. And how was your weekend?"

"I got a lot of work done," Wendy said glumly. "But the goddamned heat went off in my studio, so I had to paint in my thermals."

"Don't tell me." The stocky man whom Wendy introduced as "my painting teacher, Lenny" looked around the snack bar. "You're Wendy's roommate, the abnormal psychology major."

"I'm in philosophy," said Sylvia. "Or I will be when I declare myself."

"What does she mean 'declare herself'?" asked Lenny.

"She means" — Wendy's spoon searched the bottom of her yogurt container — "that she doesn't have to declare her major until January."

"Do you always let bureaucracies make your decisions for you?"

Sylvia stared at the hairs beneath Lenny's wedding ring, trying to figure out what bureaucracy he was talking about. (The dean, who'd wanted her to take it easy last year? Her philosophy professor, the breast lady?) She lowered her eyes.

His hand, beneath the table, stroked the inside thigh of Wendy's paint-stained dungarees.

"I've never been around a bureaucracy before," she said.

"She's very expressive," said Lenny. "You never told me you had a roommate who was expressive."

"I did so. And you said expressiveness was overvalued."

"I said 'words are shit,' sweetheart."

Wendy laughed.

Sylvia stood up. "I have to go to the library."

"At midnight?"

"The all-night study room." Sylvia waved and kept walking, wondering on the path to Dewey House if she were obliged to go to the library because she'd said she would.

She didn't have to go, she decided, opening the door to their room. She didn't have to consider going. She didn't have to consider why she hadn't considered going. She bumped the desk leg, blinked to keep the tears inside. "Jack. Where are the flannel shirts?"

Wendy came in an hour later with a Coke.

"But I didn't have to tell you," said Wendy. "Besides, you were always asleep when I got in."

Sylvia nodded.

"Also, there's his wife. She was a student here once. His student, actually. She calls every time I'm in his office. He was afraid she'd find out."

"I feel sorry for her," said Sylvia.

Wendy stared.

"Well, I do." Sylvia's eyes filled up. She looked down to find a fist. "Lenny." The fist by her ear became a telephone receiver. "Would you please come home? The washing machine is broken."

"Look, Jane." Wendy's feet went up on the desk. "Can't you wash the clothes by hand or something?"

"Diapers, Lenny?"

"You're trying!" — Wendy's feet came down — "to make me feel bad."

Sylvia closed her eyes. She pressed her fist so hard against her lips, she felt her teeth.

It was true.

She opened her eyes, prepared to nod.

The room was empty.

"If my parents call," said the note in her box the next morning, "would you please take the message and tell them I'll call back? Anyone else can get in touch at my studio. I'll be sleeping there. It's more convenient."

"If there were a verb 'to believe falsely' it would have no significant first-person indicative." Sylvia underlined the sentence, then carried Wittgenstein from the snack bar, where she'd been reading every night, looking up, periodically, for Wendy.

She took the bus to Cambridge. "We were in the snack bar," she told Jake. "And I got into an argument with her boyfriend, her man friend, whatever you call someone who's middle-aged and married. Only it wasn't exactly an argument. And she never said she had a boyfriend." She got off his bed. "Not that she was required to. Then afterwards. In our room." She shook her head. "I wouldn't have looked at what she was doing the way she did. She didn't want to be around me."

Jake held her while she wept. "I could never understand what you thought was so wonderful about her."

"You wouldn't." She pulled away. "I didn't expect you to."

He was hard-edged, factual, different from her.

She took the bus back to school. She lay face down on Wendy's bed. When it got dark, she called Cambridge. "Hello. It's me. I just wanted to make sure you were still there."

"I'm here. You just left me."

"How are you?"

"Fine."

"You can't be."

"Why can't I be?"

He sounded fine. She giggled from relief. "That's my name."

"It's about my parents." Wendy stood in the doorway. "They think I'm still living here."

It was April.

"They're coming up this weekend. They'd like to meet

you. My father especially. He considers you a force for good." Wendy grinned and stepped into the room. "It's the philosophy major. And your mother naming you after 'who is Sylvia?'"

"How does he know about that?" Sylvia put her Magic Marker down.

"I told him. Do you mind?"

She minded. She shook her head. "You want me to play 'roommate' for you."

Wendy nodded.

"But why should I?"

"You shouldn't. But I imagined" — Wendy leaned towards her — "that you might be willing to."

"When she says things, she means them. She's like somebody in a play or something." Wendy was explaining to Mr. Klein just how serious Sylvia was.

Mr. Klein turned to Sylvia. "I hope Wendy didn't cause you grief."

"Grief? Oh no. I liked her." But everyone still looked uncomfortable, so she said, "You should see her sculpture. It's wonderful. All the teachers say so. I say so."

"How nice of you to say that," said Mrs. Klein.

Mr. Klein looked at his watch. Their dinner reservations would be taken by someone else if they didn't get a move on.

"You're sure you won't join us?" Mrs. Klein stood in the doorway.

Sylvia shook her head. "I'm sorry. I have work to do."

"That's a good girl," said Mr. Klein.

Wendy returned from supper with a pastry box. "This is from my father. He was taken with you. But then you were wonderful."

Sylvia took the box. "I loved you," she said.

"We had fun," said Wendy. "Didn't we."

After One

He told me, at eleven, that he was angry at women and though he didn't blame them exactly, he'd been driven to the point where he just made himself presentable enough to get laid once in a while.

I thought he was very presentable and I wasn't surprised when I found out later in the evening that he'd been a salesman in his married life. Fabrics, he said, a very good line, beautiful patterns and no problems getting rid of the remnants.

Now he was between careers.

At one, the man who had brought us together stood up and said, "I've got to go home."

"What's the rush?" I said.

So the man sat down. Then a little while later, he stood up again. "I'm really tired," he said. This time, we let him go. Ate chicken legs and talked about David's ex-wife. All those years together, she was counting up his faults, he said. Silently accusing him. Then one day she left and took the kid with her.

"That's too bad," I said.

It wasn't worth discussing, he said. He'd forgotten the whole rotten business. He was fine now.

He looked beautiful, but horribly unhappy to me, so I told him about my ex-husband, about how eight years after I left him, we were on the phone for the first time and my husband said, "Seven and a half years ago, you wrote a letter with a sentence in it that irritated me. That's why I never answered you." "What was the sentence?" I asked. "It was typical of you," he said. "Something about our life together. Nothing straightforward, a sly dig — I forgot the exact words."

"He didn't forget," I told David. "He just didn't want to tell me. 'Maybe the next time you'll tell me,' I said. 'During our next conversation, whenever that is.' Then I hung up. I had to laugh afterwards. Because I don't forget either."

"Oh, I don't know," he said. "If she had loved me, it might be worth something. Remembering. No. I'm better off this way. I think of her as the mother of my child. That's all."

It was one thirty and I was tired, so he walked me home.

At my house, we sat on the stoop and talked about his mother. "What did she look like?" I asked.

The usual, he told me.

"Could you be a little more specific?" I said.

His mother had big tits and skinny legs, he said, and ran a dress shop in Brighton Beach and it was his grandmother who pulled him through when his mother divorced his father and married a mick, excuse him, an Irishman, excuse him, she never actually married the guy.

"That's really something," I said. "Your mother living with someone."

"Oh, she's okay. She had a right to look for love, I guess."

I got off the stoop.

He followed me up the stairs to my apartment.

"Did he beat her?" I asked at the door.

"Who?"

"The Irishman."

"Fat chance," he said.

"You're very quiet," he said as I made coffee. "Don't you ever talk?"

"I'm thinking. About your wife and your mother."

"Don't think." So we talked about the man who had brought us together. Then we ate something.

It was five. Light out. Pale and glaring. I was exhausted and we went to bed because we had to do something. He started in licking me.

"Hey," I said.

He looked up from his work.

He had a face: broad cheeks, thick nose, dark blurry eyes. "You think it's weird? My doing that?"

"Oh no. It just seems, you know, personal, and I hardly know you."

He nodded and swam up to my level of the bed to hug me. I played with the black hairs that curled all over his breast.

"You're very pretty," I said.

"What?"

"You're very handsome," I said.

"Oh. I used to be. I thought it might have gone away when I got older. It's no use to me now." He looked down my legs. "You're lovely. You're strong."

I shrugged. We kissed. First little kisses, then long ones, like breathing exercises or the crawl.

Then he went back to his licking.

"I don't want to come," I said when I was about to.

"Why not?"

"Oh, I don't know."

So he faced down again and I came.

Then I did it to him.

When he was about to come, I rolled over on my side because I don't like the taste in my mouth and I was hoping he would want to come inside me.

"More," he said. "Keep going."

He was at an odd angle when I looked at him, eyes shut, head resting on the pillow, arms outstretched, body tilted off to one side. Under water. Under glass. I leaned over and kissed him.

"What's wrong?" he said.

"Nothing's wrong."

He closed his eyes again. I went back between his legs until he came.

We both sat up against the pillows. He put his arm around me. "I don't want you to think I'm here just for this."

"That's funny."

"What's funny?"

"Well, why shouldn't you be here just for this?"

"Look," he said. "I like you. You're not pretty exactly, but your face has character." He put his hand on my breast. I moved the hand away.

"You don't like me," he said.

"I like you fine," I said, getting out of bed.

"Hey. Come on back. I want to talk to you."

I walked over to the bureau. I took a nightgown out of the drawer.

"Let me in on the secret," he said.

"There is no secret," I said, slipping the gown over my head.

He was staring out the window. "You're holding out on me," he said. "That makes me furious."

I picked my hairbrush up. I brushed my hair until it was smooth. I could see him, in the mirror, still staring out the window.

"I could kill you," he said. "Who the hell do you think you are?"

It was light out. All the way light out. "Go home," I said, turning around.

He shook his head. "Why?"

"I don't know you. You frighten me."

"Of course you know me." He was getting out of bed. "We just spent the night together." He picked his pants off the floor, zipped them, pulled his sweater over his head. Then he emerged. Dressed. Settled his sweater over his hips.

I followed him to the doorway. Watched him fumble with the lock. "Let me do it."

"Hey. Wait a second, will you?" He shook his head, leaned down, touched my forehead with his lips.

It felt nice. I reached my hand up his sleeve. The skin was warm.

"Nice," he said, touching my nightgown. Which made me

smile, because he'd touched it, thumb and forefinger getting the hang of things, like my Uncle Izzie, the garment manufacturer. Then I remembered that this man had been in fabrics. I ran to the closet and back. "Here. Look at this. It's a nineteen forties robe I got in a thrift shop. What do you think? How should I clean it?"

He felt the fabric. "Rayon," he said. "Gently — by hand."

We kissed and discussed what fabrics came out after the war. I began thinking that maybe he should stay now that I knew him a little better.

"What are you thinking about?" he asked.

"My Uncle Izzie. He used to come to our house for supper every Friday. Once he showed up with a huge box for me. I rushed to open it, but he stopped me. "Forgive me," he said. "It's nothing. Only remnants.""

"You threw them away," he said.

"I was angry. I was expecting a present."

"You were young," he said gently. "Naive."

I nodded.

"Can I stay?" he asked.

"I don't know. Let me think about it."

"You had all night to think about it," he said, opening the door. Then he peered into the darkness of the hallway, stepped across the threshold, faced me. "If I get killed out there," he said, "it'll be your fault."

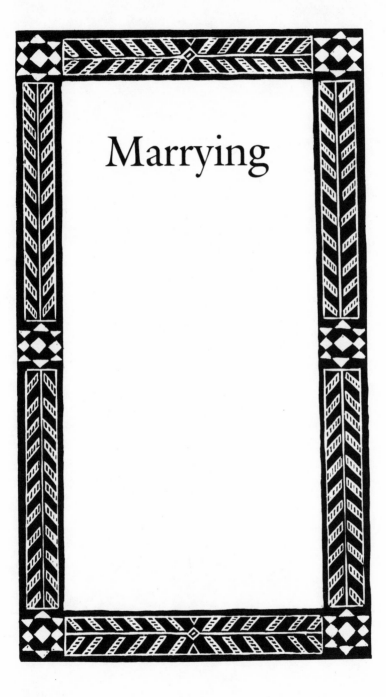

Marrying

He could feel it as he went up the steps of Low Library: that nothing he could name that sat inside him, waiting for accusations. "You're not being responsible." "You're trying to be too great." Still, he had decided he could live with it. (That IT inside him waiting sadly for accusations.) Because in real life, in the flesh and in the world and in the library, he knew he was okay. Looking at his hands, thick fingers, on the card catalog, and feeling the muscles hidden beneath his oxford blue shirt.

She had never been in love, she told the analyst. Never loved anyone. Used to love her father, but he'd disillusioned her by leaving after she was old enough to notice.

She put her hand over her eyes so that the blandness of her analyst's bookshelves (rows of analytic tracts) would be hidden when she looked for Henry James. Her lashes fluttered.

"There's something wrong with them," she said and now her hand was in her lap again. "Men, I mean. Or don't you agree with me, doctor?" Now her hand was in her lap again. Fisted, sweating, white.

* * *

He knew he was okay because he'd made a list one day in the reference room: "I am cheerful, humorous, mildly athletic, have few friends, but am forever loyal when I love."

So this thesis business had been a shock. He had had sleeping sickness every afternoon in the library and by now only his own reviews of the thesis he still couldn't find a topic for (a vast, loving, encyclopedic treatment of the rise of major league baseball) and water splashed on his face in the lavatory could wake him up.

Still, he went on taking notes through November as the air held burning leaves, not from the city, where leaves didn't burn, but from Great Neck, where he'd grown up.

She listed what was wrong with men. The lawyer, who'd offended her linguistically, not able to "get off on things," which was a direct quote from his description of some girl-friend. The poet asking for her thesis on *The Golden Bowl,* then talking, after they'd made love, about people who held back from life. Could he imagine?

But the doctor behind her didn't say a word.

And that was it for her. His knowing how sensitive she was in that area and disregarding it. "Does this drawing the line I do, seem, what's the word I want, peremptory to you? Or does it?" Waving at him from the couch. Lying like a butterfly or something light, airy, inhuman, untouch-able, untouched.

Lines on his adviser's shiny forehead when he looked at the index card with his topic on it. His adviser's Magic Marker lifted.

He couldn't read the handwriting, but his adviser's squint-eyed concentration bothered him and he could see why it had when the index card came back to him across the desk.

His *Rise of Professional Baseball* with a line through it.

The Professionalization of Baseball written underneath. He carried it out. He carried it in to point out the distinction between the topics.

His adviser nodded as he spoke, then reached with his fat hand for the card again.

The Red Wings: A Case Study in the Professionalization of Baseball (1923–26) it said when it came back to him. And forget trying to explain to this asshole the difference between the rise of something and its professionalization. Forget how narrow his epic topic had become in this man's fat hands. Just do the damned thing, he told himself.

"And that was it for me, Dr. Chein," she told the analyst. "His knowing how sensitive I was in that area and disregarding it. Of course, I felt compelled to leave him." She giggled. "It's always some line they cross. Or perhaps like *The Golden Bowl,* it is a crack. Somebody steps on it and I am finished. Done."

Waiting for her analyst's congratulations. Or his giggle. "I don't amuse you?"

But it was time to go, she saw in the hands of her own watch.

And when   I finished it, the first chapter of *The Red Wings* blah blah blah, which had appeared because he'd scribbled every day at what could always be changed, he called Abby, who'd called him, from a million years ago in Great Neck, the other day.

He would appear at her dinner party as himself again, he said. (Friendly, funny, promising, at twenty-seven without a job.) Hoping that no one else from Great Neck High would be there to notice what hadn't happened to him yet. And what, if anything, should he be bringing with him? A bottle of something?

"My best friend Abby, Dr. Chein. Not returning my call, then calling back two weeks later to ask me to bring food to her annual pre-Christmas dinner party. 'It's your party, Abby. You should bring food,' I said. I have to admit I felt triumphant when I noticed it, Abby's self-absorption. Another observation stored inside me. In case I need it. In case I need to bring it out."

It was different at the real party. For Abby was warm and generous, seating them together at the bottom of the table near the wine she said he'd brought. "Stephen's in history. Lydia's in literature. With her dissertation published and the last decent teaching job in the city."

She moved farther up the table, bending to touch shoulders, gesturing you and you, and happy to have you, while she left them to each other.

And what was that "decent teaching job" thing supposed to mean?

"Funny, you don't look composed," he said, after she'd cleared up his misapprehensions about her job by pointing out the time she'd spent on composition.

She took her hand from his water glass, then disappeared inside her body.

He was astounded. There was no light on inside her now. She might be dying for all he knew. So he rushed to promise her. "I'll make it up to you. My wretched joke. A Chinese restaurant I know. We can eat together Sunday."

Still, still. She might be dying for all he knew. Promising, promising, would his restaurant promise bring her back to life?

"Of course, for all I know nobody eats Chinese any longer," he added lifting up his fork. "The reason I wouldn't know is that my thesis keeps me out of it. I'm nursing the bugger the way some people nurse a baby or a beer."

She stared at the button on his shirt, looked blank, turned pleasant. "We've been eating together all evening, Stephen. Still, perhaps we might have second helpings Sunday." Pushing her plate away.

"I like bad jokes," he admitted at the Chinese restaurant. "I like them better than good jokes. Like the one you told at Abby's place about the second helpings."

She stared at her plate. He stared at her smooth black hair, heavy-lidded eyes, olive skin, silver earrings. He dared her to die again or to push away the plate.

She giggled, pushed the plate away. "I'll start eating too much, like my mother did. She lay in bed all day, then when I got home, she sent me out for cookies. 'The ones in the blue box. Or maybe it's the red,' she'd say. It infuriated me. Her not knowing the name of what she wanted. Her not wanting to know. But that was after my father left us. So perhaps they were related."

Her fork playing in the scallions of the *mooshoo* pork, she was daring him to what?

"Come out with me next Sunday."

At Orchard Beach the Sunday after, he pointed out his favorite spot. Close enough for the waves to wet the sand, far enough away from him to keep his toes out of it.

"I expected something more expansive," she said, hand above her eyes as if the sun were shining (it was not). "More like Truro. Or Amagansett."

"More expensive, you mean," he said. Then he was punching himself in the muscle beneath his shoulder and shouting, "You flinched. Two and a half."

He giggled.

She laughed.

"We had a good time," he insisted on the subway coming back. And felt those muscles again beneath his shoulders as hard and all right, for her face had gotten rosier, softer.

"Punching himself in the shoulder, Dr. Chein," she said. "Then he giggled. Did you ever meet a man who giggled?" She sat up before the wave inside her broke. "What do you suppose is wrong with him? He hasn't even kissed me. 'See you next week,' he says. Or maybe it's only 'see you.' No, it's 'next week.'" She lay down. "It's fortunate he hasn't pressed me to make love with him. Because his pressure would. I'd feel compelled not to gratify him. Although what *would* compel me" — the wave broke inside her. "*I* would compel me," she told the whiteness of the wall beside the couch. "Isn't that bizarre? Whose nose would I be cutting off to spite whose face?"

"Work until three," he wrote at eleven. Then he didn't get started working until two thirty, worked until four, tossed his schedule on the floor, then stepped on it as he went out and made a smudge.

That was satisfactory, he thought, on the way to visit her.

And the only way to keep himself from making up schedules he wouldn't obey was to fuck the schedules, he'd work when he felt like it.

Only he hardly ever felt like it, unless he had a date with her for afterwards. And he couldn't make dates with her beforehand, except for Sundays which had made themselves, because what if he felt like it?

The days lasted forever this winter, unless he slept a lot. The surface of his desk was full of scratches.

Feeling like it, he worked until another chapter that could always be changed appeared. Then he went to Cambridge where his older brother lived. And though he didn't feel like calling when he got home, he called because she'd be upset, then went to see her. Sitting like a little gentleman on her velvet Victorian sofa, he offered her an explanation of his conduct. "I've been in Boston. Another woman I was living with before. Who moved to Boston so I could work better. And she" — he stared at the locket between her collarbones — "could go to social work school. I didn't feel free before." Free now, he kissed her lips. Felt his body grow hard behind the softness between them.

She stood up. "The cat. I'm afraid. The couch is her spot. I'll take her to the bathroom, so she doesn't lacerate your ear."

"Don't." He grabbed her wrist. "The cat will be okay." He murmured in her ear. "What does a pussy say when she's forced to leave the room?"

"I'm appalled," she said, sitting down.

He was happy. And left the joke (which he'd made up on the spot and didn't know the answer to) because while she was appalled, he could touch bottom, then rise up easy and everything was natural after that because there was an end to it. To love, he meant. A wall to hit inside her.

She admitted it. "I like being appalled, Dr. Chein. It anchored me somehow. His joke, my disapproval. Also that other woman. She relieved me of some fear. That he was a library person, even if he is so good looking with all that dark hair, that he was like me, unlived. Now there's someone in the past to be jealous of.

The feeling? Oh, something like, if this man comes into me, not that I can't stand it. But what I can't stand — are you listening? — is this. Because what if he doesn't talk to me afterwards? And who the hell does he think I am, running off to Boston to see his girlfriend? Some piece of shit or some such thing?"

Out in the street, she thought. Maybe he's nicer than I am, because he had two parents and some brothers and sisters and lived in a house instead of an apartment.

Because her typewriter was electric and there was food in her refrigerator instead of dirty dishes like at his place, he worked at her apartment on his thesis and she brought home yellow rice and black beans and purple sausages for supper from the Chinese Cuban restaurant. "Because you made a comment the other day, about how everything was white and green in my refrigerator. Yogurt and scallions and Brie. You don't remember? It was a joke?" She was smirking, she told him, at the thought that she'd tried to please him with all this restaurant food. Like some typical woman.

After supper one evening in rainy March, he retreated. Locked the bathroom door, and read all he'd done that winter on the toilet while she did the dishes. Rising from reading draft one to flush the empty toilet, he left the manuscript on the windowsill.

The wind ruffled its pages. Would it fall out?

Then he ran a bath and stood dreaming with his hand in the water of a small boy in Great Neck standing at the paperback rack reading the jokes the author (that great and jovial man) had sprinkled all over the paperback edition for the kids.

He pulled his hand from the hot water, grabbed her towel from the rack to rub his redness with her whiteness. As he saw in the water pouring from the spout and in his hand, burning red, what he had to do to make the next draft seem normal. More cold, less hot, more mixed up, more normal.

"No, that's not how I felt, Dr. Chein. It's that the suffering he inflicted on me that he was in Boston imprinted something on my body. No, that's not it either. He makes me laugh. I, more in my life, I guess. I never liked anyone else except Abby.

"My daydreams? He's at Amherst. Surrounded by students who adore him. Mine never do. Perhaps, because as somebody said, you have to love them first. I'm lying on a chaise lounge reading Henry James as he teaches. That's all, really. There are flowers around."

"But I like your detachment," he told her. "You never flatter me. Not that you don't have expectations. But there are limits."

The wedding, in August, was at his parents' house in Great Neck.

In bed, after the wedding, she listed what she loved about his family. His father's expansiveness. "That check. That man of property business. Every tree on the lawn pointed out as if he were personally responsible for its growth and development." Plus the letters of Lytton Strachey on his mother's exquisite bed table. His brilliant brother Michael inviting them to Cambridge this fall which she adored. "But oh God, I forgot to tell you about Abby. I was fine. That is, everything was perfect until, it was my pocketbook. Abby's picking it up off the carpet and crushing it with her hands." Sobbing, she turned calm again. "If I have a baby, I don't know what that woman will try to do." The sheet pulled up until her white breasts were covered. "I'm finished with her." The sheet's hem smoothed. The gold ring on her finger turned round. "Besides, I don't need her anymore. I have you any time I want."

* * *

"I saw it in his face, Dr. Chein. Horror is too strong a word," she said. "But it was close. Love isn't everything, I realized. You have to act decent. Besides, Abby has other traits. Apart from jealousy. Loyalty for one. Liking me's another.

"I need you. Need to keep seeing you. If I have a baby, I don't know what I'll do."

He needed a model. A. J. Liebling. E. B. White. Someone sane, modest, self-deprecatory from *The New Yorker* to sit beside him while he wrote the second draft.

But nobody sane would hang around while he stayed in bed with *The Baseball Encyclopedia* all morning, then rose to go pick up her raincoat at Palatial Cleaners. And anything he wanted to bring home for supper, on her refrigerator memo, except those wretched cookies, pink and white, he bought before.

Only after supper could he sit, plowing through it, grinding it out, doing whatever you called it when one reasonable sentence after another appeared on the paper in the typewriter. Stopping to clear his throat to find his vocal cords in case he ever wished again to raise his voice.

It was her fault. His days. Those evenings. "You needn't teach those awful classes at that demeaning rate of pay," she'd said about the part-time teaching job he'd been offered that would have gotten him out of the house in the mornings. "You should finish it first. Then look for something better."

"Help," he shouted one evening.

She glanced at the *New York Post* on his lap. "If you feel the need for a break," she said softly, "we could make love, perhaps."

He kidded her afterwards about 'perhaps.' "Don't you ever say 'maybe'?"

He blamed her diction on that Henry James obsession. "Sexless wordmonger. Butter in his toothless mouth."

She looked confused. He felt bad. Because it wasn't her fault that he felt so lonely, because his wife, "entirely verbal" by her own account, never said a word to him in bed.

"But unless I hear his typewriter, Dr. Chein, I worry that he's masturbating or reading A. J. Liebling or one of those men whose work he overestimates.

"Either way I am appalled.

"He's not working to finish it. He's working not to finish it. *The Red Wings, blah blah blah* he calls it now."

All the way back to the city on the commuter train from Great Neck, he listened to her criticize his family. "Your father. The great man junk dealer. Acting as if he'd created the world. Your mother. Criticizing everyone. Treating me — I'm not the maid, you know. Not even your sainted brother, I notice, asks me how my work is going these days."

He asked her how her work was going.

"Fine. It always goes fine. I'm finishing an article on Maisie. *What Maisie Knew,*" she added, as if he didn't.

"Good. I'm glad. Mine is going badly.

"I want a baby," she said looking out the dirty Long Island Railroad window onto the houses that lined the tracks.

* * *

What he liked best about their baby decision, he said, grasp-
ing her hand, was the way it made no sense considering
their, no, his, situation. "That's not a joke. That's a feeling."

She took her hand away to place it on her belly. "I had no
room I thought, for anyone else inside me. But some generosity I learned from you. Not that I expect to be a cow like
those other women in the natural childbirth classes." Smiling and shrugging, as he got out of bed to get his sphinx box,
which had his manuscript in it. He hoped she'd be smiling,
when he came back, but she was propped like a queen
against her pillows.

He knelt by the bed. "Draft one," he said, reaching up to
lay the box in her hands. "Was sprawling. Incoherent. Full of
life." He waited for her to giggle, then rose when she did
not. "While this thing is so damned tight assed, I'm afraid no
one can make it out." A faint smile on her pale face. Pleased
with something. How terrified he'd been, perhaps. "So I
thought I'd take another stab after you looked at it."

Her finger on his little set of pages.

"What kills me about those natural childbirth classes," he
said, trying not to look or see, "is all that liberal bullshit. No
pain, for Christ's sake. If you breathe correctly."

His fist raised itself.

"If God had wanted." Smiling.

She had it made inside her. Nothing further would be
asked of her.

"A joke about God, of course," he said. "But look at it this
way. If there's something wrong with it, I wish you'd
tell me."

* * *

It was this draft, she said. This was the place to stop at. A few transitional phrases to add, of course, but she'd been pleasantly surprised by his humor. Although she shouldn't be. But certain unintelligible spots. She'd marked them. Her guess: "You're too shy to be forthright."

But the noises in his head were too loud for him to hear her, so thanking her courteously for helping him, he picked up the sphinx box and carried it to the bathroom. Where he couldn't remember where it went normally.

He put it on the window ledge and ran the bath.

They cut her belly to get Elizabeth out. He thought of veal, lamb chops, ham, then went down, went out, like the refrigerator light on the Brie. It wasn't the sight, for he was out of the room when they did it, but the idea. When he got back in to where she lay, he had a daughter. Screaming at him. But until he got to play with her, she thought she was Lydia's child only. That it was Lydia's competence that made Elizabeth come out a girl, instead of somebody more like him.

Lydia also felt cheated. If she'd been better about the pain, she'd asked, would they have let her have the baby?

She had the baby, he'd insisted. Hugging her to make it real, after the fact. Placing the baby in her arms.

But she'd insisted too. That caesarean didn't come from Caesar and Caesar didn't come from one. Which was a joke. She glared at him. About all kinds of things, ambition.

Then giggling, she went back to teaching and came home with healthy cookies that he felt compelled to eat. While she went to bed and fed the baby he had given her.

*   *   *

Three weeks later, he found it. The joke he should have made. And slipping this thesis, not good enough, but as good as he could make it, into a manila envelope, he made it. And it was "Who wants a little Caesar running around a one-bedroom apartment?"

Marking the face of the yellow envelope with his adviser's address, he closed the hole in back with silver fasteners and hung Elizabeth in front in a Snugli around his neck.

Some things get better, he thought, carrying them to the post office. In minor ways, at least. As the envelope went easy into the slot marked MANHATTAN ONLY and he looked up to find black and white criminals on the post office walls, then down to find Elizabeth, not entirely adorable, in her Snugli round his neck.

"I wouldn't be writing you, Dr. Chein, if I weren't devastated. While it's not entirely my fault, I'm afraid that Elizabeth will be schizophrenic. Or hate me, for being so ungiving when she was young."

She tried remembering the source of her devastation. "Burton White, he's from Harvard, so I can't help believing him, claims it's my detachment that has ruined her. That and my reading *The Wings of the Dove* while she was breast-feeding. It's White's book, not White himself, I understand this from *The First Three Years of Life*."

Giggles from the living room.

"Stephen won't help me. He lies playing with 'my child,' he calls her, which is indicative. I know he hasn't looked for work because the help wanted section of *The Times* is pristine. The ink comes off on my fingers when I touch it."

She rose from her desk, because she couldn't write a psychoanalyst the shameful truth. Stephen had a job, worked nights, was paid like a graduate student, was a failure with a fatal flaw and he'd gone on and on, no matter what she wanted.

She reached him in the living room and said, "The pay is demeaning on that job," to her husband playing with his child upon the floor. Meanwhile, she saw how little any of it had touched her, the husband, the child, the life.

It took some time for him to understand. That she was talking about the teaching job he'd found in Bensonhurst, part-time.

Middle-aged women who lie in bed all day, she cried, looking down at him. Rising for his class at night as if he were a God something. While she — dragging herself to school every morning. While he — lying on the floor playing with Elizabeth like a child, then appearing nights, like a werewolf, for these women.

He stood amazed. He stood amazed, as he got up. Because she sounded mad, he meant crazy, and tumbling into her words, as if into seawater, he heard "Bensonhurst, demeaning," and shouted "Brooklyn," as if to locate Bensonhurst for both of them.

Because Brooklyn was where he'd grown up and what a wonderful place to grow up in it was and moving to Great Neck did no good, he shouted. His mother hated it. Hated the spot. Even after his father had spent a fortune trying to please her.

"You have a job," he told her, feeling freer as he moved

closer to her. "Do whatever you want to. There are certain restrictions on me. My integrity," he added. "I do not choose to join the world."

He stepped down. His desert boot upon her instep, his weight upon her sole. He took his foot away as if he'd paid her back for something.

He watched her leave him.

He heard the words he'd said about the world and his integrity, how ridiculous they sounded.

That shadowy IT inside him flickered and went out. And in exchange, behind the door that shut, he found a woman he was married to, whoever she was in real life, however this life he was caught in, turned out.

So after Dr. Chein had promised: 'IF YOU LEAVE YOUR NAME, NUMBER, AND ANY MESSAGE ON THE MACHINE, I'LL CALL BACK,' she sat in the Chock Full O'Nuts drinking coffee and thinking about her mother in the huge white bed in the afternoons with something moving from the blueness of her painted eyelid to the red nail on the finger she shook. "Now, darling. Why work so hard at everything? Just go outside and let me sleep." Fat arm across her forehead, she closed her eyes.

Tears got brushed away as she got up to pay the check. Forget the message to Dr. Chein. Forget the words she'd found for Stephen. "So fail. So teach in Bensonhurst forever. Why should it bother me?" Not asking, for she knew it was her right, she'd pick up Elizabeth and start playing and having fun.

* * *

Six weeks into the semester in Bensonhurst, he came home and said, "I can't go on like this. Teaching *The Rise of the American Empire* and taking shit they wouldn't hand me at the post office. If I can stay home in the evenings when you take Elizabeth, I'll turn my thesis into a trade book and we'll be rich."

"Oh no," she said. "You can't. You won't. Hanging around the house in your pajamas. You have a child now. You can't jeopardize whatever income you — You can move on when the semester is over. I can't, writing takes forever, we can't afford it."

"I can't move on. Every other teaching job is in Dallas. Or Taiwan. You have the last decent job in this city, Lydia."

She made a mouth and left him. Because he sounded as if she'd stolen it from him. She came back (in the elevator) and he followed her to the kitchen and she poured herself a glass of juice and handed it to him and poured another. Drank. "We can't both be afraid. I've decided to live here," she said quietly.

"How come we didn't break a glass at our wedding?"

She didn't answer his question. Which was, as usual, flip and serious. Because they'd tried, that was the funny situation, to step on the glass, but it had rolled, rolled, rolled, until somebody, some kid, flower girl or ring bearer, had stepped on it instead.

Then crunch.

Shards everywhere.

They'd laughed, thank God. Or he had. Maybe that was what he was remembering. And meanwhile, in her silence

now, he'd looked out the dirty kitchen window at the wall
where there were names sprayed in giant letters, even if you
couldn't read them. Then relieved, he put the juice glass on
the kitchen table and thought that she had probably seen
it — (what was wrong with him) — and IT was this: he was
afraid and having seen it, she preferred to live with him and
it than be so lonely.

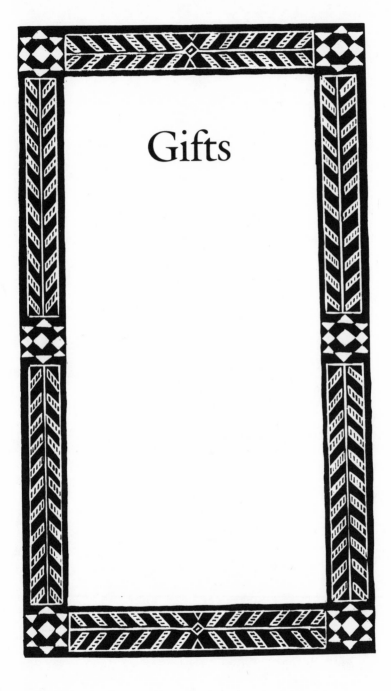

Gifts

My mother tells me that a gift will arrive for me by mail, from Macy's. I try to thank her, but can't, because I've asked her not to send me gifts anymore, clothes especially. I'm thirty. I've got a closet full of gifts from her, have never really dressed myself. My mother is sixty-five. We're in the dressing room of the municipal pool together. Her back is to me. She's squatting. Piling clothes into her locker. She turns around, stands, looks up at me. Her small pointed face is hopeful. Her breasts droop. She's naked.

"It's a shirt," she says.

So you asked her not to send you gifts, I think. She wants to send you a shirt from Macy's. Let her send you a shirt from Macy's.

"You can always return it," she says, after a while.

"Okay. I'll return it if it isn't right."

"Fine," she says. "I'll return it for you. It's easier for me to get to Macy's. I'm not so busy." She pulls her bathing suit up, settles her breasts inside. "I would have gotten it for myself," she adds, "if they had it in my size or in a different color."

I put one foot into the leg of my leotard.

"You're not taking a shower before you go in?"

"I never do. Look, Ma, I probably won't want to return it. You have wonderful taste, usually."

"It looked like you," she says. "Simple. Not severe. But I could be wrong."

We start for the pool. The water is warm, chlorinated. She breaststrokes. I crawl. She favors her right side, because her left hip was broken in a car accident and never mended. I favor my left, because my bad basketball knee won't kick. We swim back and forth, lose each other. I look around. She's holding on to the ladder, dangling. I swim up to her.

"Are you okay?"

"Fine. I was watching you. You're a strong swimmer."

"So are you."

"Grandma was stronger."

We used to watch from the beach. Grandma at the water's edge. Mrs. Handelman on one side, Mrs. Scheineman on the other. Black woolen tank suits wrinkling around their old ladies' thighs, the three women chatting, bending, scooping water from the lake, sprinkling water on their bosoms, rubbing water into their wrists, elbows, shoulder blades, like perfume, then crack — Grandma was gone, wading into the lake, thighs carrying her out, past the rope, past the lifeguard's whistling objections, breaststroking across the lake, then back to us again, bunioned feet covered with sand, water dripping on our blanket as she reached for the bathrobe that my mother held out to her, wrapped it around her, waited like a wrestler for the lifeguard to approach: "What's he so afraid of, that boy in the high chair? I'll be drowned? I can't go out alone? An old lady like me?"

"I loved her," says my mother. "But I could never talk to her." She lets go of the ladder. Her legs stir up the waters behind her. Her freckled arms part the waters in front of her. She detours around a group of splashing children, swims swiftly down the center of the pool, then lifts herself to the concrete edge at the other end, dangles her legs in the water, kicks, smiles.

I wave.

We meet in the dressing room.

I admire her haircut. She likes the way I wrap my towel around my head. We start for the subway. She's tired now. Her hip hurts her. At the turnstile, she takes two tokens out of her pocketbook. "Here. For you."

"Never mind. I can get one."

"You'll have to stand in line." She points to the token booth.

I take the token. Offer her fifty cents.

She shakes her head. "The price is terrible," she says, slipping her token into the turnstile. The machine clanks and turns, noisy, but functional. Then it's my turn.

Inside the subway car, I find an empty seat for her. She holds the pole. "Save the seat for someone who needs it," she says. I hold the same pole, thinking longingly of France, where subway sitting is regulated by the state, where the *mutilés de guerre* go first, then *les personnes âgés, les femmes enceintes, mutilés ordinaires.*

"For my sake," I say, pointing to the seat.

She sits down.

I grab the strap above her. She wipes her eyes. I lean down to see what the matter is. She says the chlorine in the pool makes her eyes hurt. It's not right, what they do to the waters, the elements.

I'm sorry about her eyes, I say, but the pool is better than nothing, better than what most people have.

She's grateful, she supposes.

My stop is next.

At home, there's a package from Macy's waiting.

Unwrapped, it's the same shirt I bought four years ago, got tired of, hung on a tree outside, watched my neighbor take home with her.

No, it's not the same shirt, I see, unpinning it, unfolding it, slipping the cardboard out, holding it against me. Same material. Different cut. Softer. Not so severe.

I call my mother to tell her.

She says, "I thought it looked like you, but I wasn't sure. I worried."

"Don't worry, Ma," I say.

She's quiet.

"I love it," I say.

"I did okay?"

"You did fine, believe me."

"I'm surprised," she says. "I didn't expect it to arrive so soon."

Now we're both quiet. I follow the telephone wires across town and back. "I don't want to run up your phone bill," she says. "I'm getting off."

She gets off. The line is free again. I stand, listening to nothing. A few minutes later, I'm dialing my brother in California. I want to hear his voice. See what he sounds like. "Hello," he says. "Is that you?"

Story

Once there was a woman who wished for a child. She wished for a child soon, because she was thirty-three, and she wished for a girl child because she was alone and thought a girl could grow up to be a woman without a man around, but a boy should have a father.

"Don't you agree?" she asked her friend Marvin, who sat rolling a joint on her bed.

Marvin had never thought about the question.

The main problem, though, the woman Marilyn went on, was that if you told the man, he'd feel responsible for the child. But who'd want someone you'd lie to as the father?

Marvin lit the joint and leaned back against her pillows.

He'd never thought about that either, he said, smiling like the sun.

So it wasn't, she reflected, joining him in bed, as if she hadn't warned him.

Still, Marvin looked surprised, three months later, when he got back from California and found Marilyn in the waiting room of a hospital that was known for its midwifery program. "Hello, hello," they said. Then he explained that a woman reporter was expected later on, but that his newspaper wanted coverage of the midwifery program from both angles, as she, explaining nothing, lifted her blue shawl from her rounded belly and laid it upon her shoulders.

Then they left together, because they were both leaving, and took the subway together, because they lived in the same neighborhood, and stopped for coffee, because he felt wrecked and she wanted his opinion of the midwifery program. Which was, he whispered hoarsely, fine.

Weeks passed. Marilyn's job as a planner for the city got abolished. If at first the loss seemed terrible, she told Marvin when she met him at the library, she'd gradually come to see the blessing that twenty-six weeks of unemployment could be to begin her child's life upon.

Marvin flushed. He'd been thinking about her. But every time he'd been about to call, something came up. Still, if he'd known she was unemployed. And if she ever needed money. He meant it. "Ever in the next twenty years" — with tears in his eyes. "I mean it, Marilyn."

Now Marilyn moved from the return desk, but after she'd checked out her meatless recipe book, he was still turning the paperback rack, so they walked down the dark circular staircase to the revolving door, where she paused as his briefcase was examined for stolen books. Then they each pushed a section of the door until they saw the sunshine.

And she invited him for lemonade with mint from her mother's garden in Minneapolis and he left his book, *A Beginner's Guide to Carpentry,* on her bed and they separated again.

The problem, thought Marvin, on his way back to Marilyn's to pick his book up, was that he liked Marilyn. Say, if he hadn't known her. Say, if they'd met at some party some Saturday night. He'd be wanting to sleep with her and maybe even live with her, especially if she'd gotten pregnant and wished to keep the child.

But she hadn't gotten pregnant. She had wished for the child in the first place. And the worst part was not being able to discuss it with a friend whose opinion he respected, because that friend was Marilyn.

When he reached Marilyn's place, she was restless. So they walked to the pier, then to his place, where he lit a joint, then killed it for the baby's sake, and turned on the TV. And after Ernest Borgnine, from the deck of a cargo boat, said, "I believe in God, President Roosevelt and the Brooklyn Dodgers," Marvin turned the set off and Marilyn said, "I want you to know I'm a responsible human being and I never do anything I haven't thought through."

"I know, I know," said Marvin.

He starts towards her, tears in his eyes and his arms outstretched.

I watch, feeling desolate, as if some wish will be lost to me forever, when they reach each other.

Behind me, there are noises. Like the wings of an angel or an acetate housedress, they're at my shoulder before I turn to face the source.

It's my mother.

I pull my sheet from my typewriter, place it face down on the glass-topped desk, answer her question before it gets asked. "They're about to go to bed. For a second time."

My mother's eyes close. Her spirit starts down the circular staircase inside her. She tests each step with her toes before she puts her foot down. Does Marilyn need to go to bed with him again? Or does she wish to?

Then clasping her hands to make wishes and needs come together, she says, "If it happens once more, Marvin will be moving in with Marilyn and building bookshelves or even a loft bed. Something with the space for a cradle underneath."

I stand, gather my sheets, say I'm going home.

My mother reminds me that I'm typing at her apartment because Con Edison has cut the current on my block. Any moment, my father will appear. Borscht awaits us. Scallions swim in a deep red sea around the new potato rocks. "And there's corn bread. The chewy kind. Like rye."

The pleasure she'll take when what she's made gets eaten spreads across her face like sunlight.

I follow her from the bedroom I've been using as a study to the living room where we will eat. "Next time, would you invite me, please, so I can make up my mind before the food gets cooked?"

"You always stay." She looks surprised.

Do I always stay? I set three stainless steel spoons around three soup bowls. Or does she only say I stay to get me to?

My mother asks if borscht, Greek salad, and the corn rye I'm placing in the hollow belly of a woven dove will be enough or should she run to the deli for a whitefish.

"Enough," I say.

My father appears.

"Oh, it's you." Tears of family feeling fill his eyes. He pulls his pants from beneath his belly, then sits at the head of this circular table to work his ruminative way from his Talmudic past in Europe to his life as a lawyer in this land.

"Business, labor, crime, real estate, divorce," recites my mother, to remind him of the cases he refused, while waiting in his office for something constitutional to appear.

My father, uneasy, turns to tell me how astonished he was to receive his retirement notice from the unemployment insurance board where he's worked since my conception. He'd been too busy thinking about time, he says, to notice the passage of years as they swam by.

"I've been thinking," says my mother, "of retiring too." Silvery glints of irony swim like fish behind her bifocals as she peers at the borscht in my father's bowl. The phone rings. She runs to get it. I wait for my father to inquire in her absence about my brother, the only mortal who can move him from his ruminations or my mother's soup.

My father looks up at me. "I'll be studying comparative religion at the New School. What are you doing?"

"That was Marilyn." My mother returns with a bulging bag from Best and Company. "Calling about the baby clothes. I forgot to tell you. That after I met her in the park last week, I couldn't fall asleep. Poor child. No father for her child. It wasn't until I turned the late show on that I remembered. Some boat carrying supplies to Murmansk during the war." She pats the bag. "Your father was asleep." Smiling like the sun, she spreads the handles. "Look," she says triumphantly.

I look.

The velvet hat my father used to pray beneath in Poland sits unused on a mountain of baby things.

"For you." She fingers the crown of the yarmulke, casts her eyes down piously on what she's gathered for the child I never had. "Everything else is for Marilyn's baby."

My father's spoon taps his empty borscht bowl.

I look west, towards the sunset, and hear the tap, tap, tap, of my hatless, bookless brother's carpenter's hammer in California.

I rise to pick the bag up, bend to kiss my mother's cheek, and touch my lips to my father's broad forehead.

He follows me to the doorway. "You're leaving so soon?"

Twenty flights later, the doorman acknowledges my presence and departure in a nod.

I walk west, prepared for action, that is, for thought and a return to Marvin and Marilyn, who are having trouble meeting. For if, as people in my mother's life, they often fail to find the words to clothe their actions in, they are readers in my story, as we can see by their meeting at the library and Marvin leaving his book on Marilyn's bed and the bookshelves my mother has him building in an apartment he doesn't live in yet. And as readers, they know that if a first time in bed might be impulsive, and a second, an attempt to justify the impulse, a third will form a pool, where, thoughtful or impulsive, they will swim like the fish in my mother's eyes, until they find a resting place.

So while Marvin can still bump into Marilyn at the library, he may not be going in her direction afterwards. Or she may not have time to stop for coffee because someone has said there are baby clothes for sale at the Temple Emmanuel bazaar.

I've reached the Laundromat. The same Laundromat, I

decide, standing in the weeds that grow before the window, where Marvin met Marilyn for the third and final time.

Marvin stood where I stand, watching Marilyn through the glass, while Marilyn sat, watching her overalls tumble in the belly of the machine. Then he walked through the open door and dropped his bag off his shoulder. He was pleased, he said, to see her. Really pleased, he said, surprised by the conviction in his voice. Marilyn likewise, but more self-contained, invited him to join her for a Sprite outside, where they sat on two milk crates, one tree in an iron girdle before them, turning colors, dropping leaves.

Then Marilyn, flushed by the heat within, would explain how well she was doing and how interesting this experience was turning out to be.

"Look, Marilyn, I want to live with you," said Marvin, who'd spent weeks avoiding that thought, locking himself, when it appeared, in the bathroom with the *Columbia Journalism Review*. But this Friday evening he'd lifted his laundry bag off the hook instead and carried it to Marilyn, whom he'd glimpsed behind the glass the Sunday before, sitting with her eyes cast down.

"I'll have to think about it," said Marilyn, dragging his sense of his body back to the milk crates, where his thought hovered like a dove above her crown of braids. Standing (because he couldn't stand her lack of spontaneity), he sat again (to avoid his wish to kneel) and said "for sure" because he was sure that the child was as real inside her as if it had been wished for in words by them both.

Besides, pulling his pants proudly over his belly, why shouldn't he wish for what he'd made, cherish what he'd created, own what already belonged to him? Since one way or another, they both had to eat, he said, why not go back to her place?

They leave to pick up chicken breasts.

I shift my bag to my other hand and watch Marilyn, exhausted, climb the ladder to her loft bed, where she lies, ruminating about whether a child whose mother ruminates forever shouldn't have a father who never thinks to bounce him on her lap.

I'm falling asleep, thinks Marilyn as the current inside her gets cut and the light she would need to swim back to her reflection fails and the parents are left in darkness, exchanging characters, while the child exchanges sexes with the lap.

Below her, Marvin's hammer taps. He's looking for the beams to put the brackets in, so that the bookshelves can go up.

It isn't a question of shoulds, thinks Marilyn, waking in the night. My child does have a father. How have I forgotten him? Tugging at the frayed binding of the comforter she's carried from her mother's house, she turns towards Marvin, who's climbed the ladder to lie beside her.

His hand moves towards her belly as I carry her question down the block. ST. ANNE'S, says the cornerstone of the church I stop before.

Her child did have a father, I tell the statue of a woman with a child on her lap. How had she forgotten him?

The statue's eyes are cast down upon my shopping bag. I let my hand descend to my father's hat that lies beyond me, then raise my eyes again.

The sky darkens above the harbor that my father sailed into.

My hand comes up empty.

My feet move through the dusk until I reach the place the statue sits. Careful not to touch her son, I stand on tiptoe before her.

My lips of flesh touch her lips of marble.

My body stays behind, as I rise to what my lips have kissed, then fall into the darkness inside her.

Bliss surrounds me. I swim in circles in a chamber full of seawater that grows as I grow. Then, suddenly as sleep, my bliss gets interrupted and my chamber stops growing as I grow on.

My chamber has become a cell. My cell has become a passageway. The walls of my passageway have become alive and I am pushed by what's behind me to swim forward, towards the light the statue's downcast eyes deny.

I cast my eyes down to find a shopping bag upon concrete. Then I kneel before its mouth to bring the hat up, place it on my crown of braids and look around.

Before me sits the statue of a woman in a shawl with her son upon her lap. Behind her stands a church. And behind the church, the sea my father sailed across with the hat he wore to help him see beyond himself, without mistaking what he'd seen for what he'd made.

I put the hat on my head, then look behind me to find the son still smiling. Then I start down the block to Marilyn's with a bag that's so much lighter I can climb six flights of stairs and touch a wind chime before reflecting that only five flights are permitted without an elevator by the housing code.

Fragments of glass strike each other and reverberate. MAR-ILYN LEWIS, says the engraved portion of the calling card beneath a thumbtack on a wooden door. MARVIN EPSTEIN, says the Magic Marker scrawl below.

The door opens.

I lower my eyes from the shiny dark hair upon the blue denim shoulders of a woman and find a man's hand beside her.

I reach beyond myself.

The bag reaches Marvin.

He shakes his fingers to get the fear out, then reaches in.

A receiving blanket takes the shape of the arm he's stretched to reach it. His hand holds a crib mirror before his face.

Silvery fish swim in his eyes as he searches his reflection for the father his child will see. Then his free hand goes below, but before I see what's in it, the bag's been handed to Marilyn and a tower of books has been built in the hands before her belly.

I turn my head to find Marilyn looking simple, then awesome, then holy.

"Look, Marilyn." Marvin holds up the Vita jar. "Herring in sour cream."

Marilyn looks at the face that's come from behind the glass.

Lips of flesh smile inside the halo of his beard.

Marilyn lowers her eyes, grins, drops the tower.

I kneel before the woman who's knelt to pick up the books I owned as a child and kiss the cheek of the girl I knew at Barnard.

My hat falls off.

"Take them." Marilyn points to fairy stories, Bible stories, stories of gods and goddesses beyond the sea. "You can come over and read to us."

I pick the books up and take my hat in my hand as Marilyn leans forward to kiss my forehead. We both rise. Marvin holds his hand out. "Thank your mother for the gifts," he says.

I take his hand and say my father should be thanked as well for being so preoccupied that my brother got to leave his hat behind and my mother got to hand it to me and I got to wear it on my way to their apartment, where their child will live, blessed by unemployment checks, and preceded by the stories of their lives.

Then we stand, holding hands, brothers and sisters in a real world of wishes and things to be, until Marilyn opens the door behind her and everyone waves goodbye and six flights turn to five going down and the sidewalk appears before I've imagined it.

I'm thirty-seven, childless, with a bag of books in one hand and a hat in the other.

I turn my own corner, climb my stairs, stand before my door and jiggle my key until the iron rod behind begins to stir. Then pushing to enter, I flick a switch to find the current back and welcome myself to my apartment with the lights on.

Then I sit before my typewriter to plan a wedding for planful Marilyn and unconscious Marvin and the child who will appear among us. And if the person I've called up to do the ceremony isn't certain how to wed them, at least she's got a hat that lets her reach beyond herself to find the words. And with the labor redivided and two parents for each child, she can reach beyond the words to find a breakfast for the wedding guests: blood red burgundy and chewy ruminative rye and between them, a whitefish sits — golden skinned as the gods we dress our wishes in, with eyes as dark as looking forward to what's not. Then I turn my head to find the whole and find the body, shaped by the limitations that make us need each other, the needs that make us wish to come together and be whole.

Blue
Spruce

Once upon a time, a poor orphan lived alone in a forest near Riga. The boy's mother had been eaten by wolves and the boy's father had run away with a Russian ballerina. Friendless, parentless and penniless, the boy in the forest cut wood, which he carried on his back into Riga to sell. One day a drunken policeman taunted him, calling him "Juden" and worse. The boy knocked the policeman out, then ran and hid beneath a bridge, burning logs to keep himself warm and catching carp to eat, while he built a raft under cover of darkness. Then he sailed downstream, abandoning the raft to climb mountains and cross borders and in one way or another make his way to where the ocean was, which he sailed across. On the other side, he reached a city on a hill, which was Troy, New York. There he worked his way up into a king of sorts.

Everyone has objected, at one time or another, to this version of my grandfather's origins.

My mother: "An orphan? He told you that, Natalie? He was no more orphan than I was. Certainly, I grant you this, he had no parents. Lots of people lost them in those days. Death was more prevalent then, even in this country. Take a look at the graveyards — young people, babies, it always makes me weep. But Papa had sisters in Trenton, an aunt in Philadelphia. He didn't *have* to be so solitary."

My father: "I come from the same part of the world as he did. Poland, Russia, these are made-up distinctions, after the fact. This is small-town life we're talking about. Nobody knocked out a policeman in Riga and lived to boast about it. No Jew in those days even *thought* about doing such a thing. Somebody might overhear the thought and report it. And another thing: no orphan learned Hebrew, which he pretended not to know. I caught him reading the Gemara once. Rabbis, religion, these I understand him being angry at. Even that monkey business — leaving open his store on Yom Kippur, just to make his neighbors, well, unhappy. But why would anyone hate a language? What was that about?"

"But where did Grandpa get the nails to build that raft?" asked my brother Jonathan on the phone from California. Carefully casual, belying the intensity of the yearnings Grandpa planted in his soul, my blond blue-eyed brother mentioned that Grandpa was blond and blue-eyed too. So maybe there was a Russian ballerina somewhere. Someone tall, slim, graceful, Russian instead of Jewish, rooted in land and lifted into air, embodied, transcendent, different from us. "It's impossible, for sure. A Russian lady from the Bolshoi marrying some impoverished Jewish woodcutter? Still, look how crazy I am about skiing and what a maniac you were about dance, Natalie. You know, we're physical. So where did that come from?" Shame filled the silence between

us. Atonement for his yearnings, his explanations, his grandfather's character and his own, which are so similar. "I mean,
get this: a wolf who was really a ballerina waltzing into some
forest where Grandpa's father was crouched in a cave before
a fire and —"

"But there *were* caves in Russia. Don't you remember,
Jon?" I interrupted. "Those weddings we went to with relatives with numbers on their arms, who'd hidden from the
Germans in one. Or was that Poland? But never mind the
caves. This is my point. Somebody, maybe Grandpa, used to
talk about his life before he came here and get tears in his
eyes: 'We were so poor we had no shoes,' he'd wail. Well,
they must have had shoes, I've decided. Old shoes, shoes
with holes in them, rags around their feet, I saw pictures at
the Jewish Museum. But some sort of shoes, especially in the
wintertime. So maybe he was saying how poor he'd been,
how poor he felt, compared to us in America, his grandchildren."

"I'll buy that," said Jonathan, hanging up.

So there'd been loneliness in that forest, but my grandfather
had had relatives. There'd been yearnings, ambitions, but
nobody had married a ballerina. There'd been hunger and
fear, wolves and policemen, but nobody had gotten eaten or
knocked out. For my grandfather, who came from the same
part of the world as my father, had the same attitude towards
the facts — that they are interchangeable, changeable gar-
ments that exist so naked unchangeable truths can walk
among us and be dressed.

What's left of my grandfather's Russia, you may have

noticed, after everyone has put their two cents in, is a pine forest. For no one has ever questioned the existence of that forest near Riga, although no one but my grandfather has ever been anywhere near the spot. Beside the pine forest, I found this thought: that my grandfather's version of his Russian boyhood must have grown out of this feeling that the real story wasn't good enough.

My mother: "My father did well in Troy. He had Mama, and us, that store, and that partner, Segesta, the best sausage maker in the city. Ask anyone. Jake loved his livelihood. Driving pell-mell at three in the morning to Schoharie County where the farmers were. I have to say it, I was his favorite. I looked like him, they said. He'd take me with him in the truck. It was still dark. The farmers were still sleeping. We'd go into the orchards by ourselves. He'd pick an apple, twist the stem, bite down, then spit it out. Pronounce the name: Macintosh, Northern Spy. The names still have this glamour for me. Pronounce his judgment, rotten, ripe. Not good enough for Stern and Segesta. I worried, can you believe the way a child's mind works, that he'd throw me away if I displeased him. Had worms or got mushy.

"When he bought the land at Lake Mohican, I was the first to see it. Pines all over the property, which I must point out he cut down on an impulse, like everything else he did. He was going to build the bungalow himself. Only everything he wanted was impossible. He wouldn't measure and he wouldn't wait for the paint to dry. Everything had to go fast, according to his wishes, roofs and porches, as well as people. Mama begged him to hire a helper. The helper pleaded with me, a little girl, to get him out of there. It was the best land, said Papa. Why not the best bungalow?

"You know that other people's camps had friendly names. Welcome Inn, Gremlin's Lodge, things like that. Papa's camp was named IF. 'If you like it, you can stay. If you don't, get the hell out,' was how he explained it. Now what kind of attitude is that? Other people's bungalows were better built. They had more land, a larger lot."

My grandfather would have approved of and been enraged by my mother's judgment of his lot. More is better, but mine is best, he said, asserting his supremacy by banging one fist into the other while he peeked over his shoulder to see what his neighbors had gotten for themselves.

The redwoods dwarf the pines in California. My brother's dictum on the envy and ambition question arrived on a postcard early in this week I've spent alone at the bungalow whose higgledy-piggledy interior is dark, shadowed by two tall spruces in the yard.

> Land is expanse, offering solitude, perspective, etc. What Grandpa had in Lake Mohican was a medium-sized, working-class, immigrant's lot.
>
> Love,
> Jonathan

On the other side of his postcard were the Sierras looking lofty. Jonathan has hiked up mountains that make my grandfather's Adirondacks look like molehills. "Okay, land is expanse and etc.," I wrote back on a Kodachrome of Lake Mohican. "But aren't expanse and etc. still lots?"

He'll get my point. We've practiced. We've shared the pleasures of the word, like apples in the mouth, since my grandfather, in a gravelly Russian voice, introduced them to us:

He's the biggest crook in six counties.

The Republicans got the tombstone vote.

A nothing, a nobody, he watered the cream for a living in Buffalo.

Shears Robust. It's where they sell the lawn mowers from a book.

The World's Serious.

Your father, the man who can't hammer a nail through butter.

My grandfather, I add to the list, the man who sandwiched his mistakes in English between two jokes.

The store flourished. My grandmother worked beside him, while his daughters studied music and gave recitals: O Wild Red Rose, my mother dressed in petals sang. My grandfather emerged from the bungalow on weekends with an ax in his hand, muscle and shoulder blade beneath the strings of his undershirt, gray work pants strapped with a belt around his stringy body. He looked a little like a wolf himself, though not a ballerina. Wood chips flew as his activity spoke out for him: Don't just sit there. Do something, make something, be something, someone.

"So I climbed mountains," said my mother, "took elocution lessons, went to Montreal to study French. And when I dared to spend a summer with your father in New Jersey, I got these postcards: 'Go ahead, stay wherever you want to, but there's nothing better than Lake Mohican, not even Paris, France, or Leningrad. And don't come back to this place too soon, because we're full up with guests.' "

Filial, loyal, dying to leave him, she returned the next summer with a husband who came from the same part of the world as her father did.

"Jake was already old, blind in one eye. It must have been the diabetes." It's my father speaking now. "Every time, well, I didn't really mind him nudging my croquet ball into the ragweed, but your mother, that's another story. This kind of monkey business drove her wild. Then on Sunday, we had a game and again, that nudge through the wicket and so he won, just before we were on our way home. So your mother started in on him. But this time into the Buick — right, Helene? — he jumped. Driving a hundred miles an hour down that stony Creek Road to Troy where he handed his store over to Segesta. I mean it. Gave it to this younger fellow, very honest. Shouted, 'Go ahead and take it all away from me. You've been stealing me blind right along.' Segesta pleaded with Jake to let him pay for it. Later, the fellow brought money to your grandmother on the sly.

"Now what kind of sense does that make? When it's his daughter he's mad at. Or me maybe, for marrying her. And that store, how he loved it. Another thing I never understood: if Jake wanted to retire, why not take his half of the store and sell it, like normal people do? What was all the rage about? I don't believe in Freud. But I think the reason that your mother hated him was syphilis. He got it from the

Polish girl, who cleaned for them. In those days, they thought it was hereditary."

"I was pregnant," from my mother. "We lived way out in Bensonhurst, in Brooklyn. Papa was in the hospital uptown. Mama had just died. He was in Flower and Fifth Avenue or some such place. It took an hour and a half on the BMT to get there, but I went to see him every day. Troy was a one-horse town as far as medicine went, said Papa. Really, I think he was ashamed. His hands shook. I felt sorry for him, so I stood, big as a house, on the subway to go and visit. Nobody offered me a seat.

"At the hospital, he kept two lists. The people who'd come to see him or sent cards on one list. The ones who had forgotten on the other.

"Maybe I had to go to the obstetrician. I've forgotten why I didn't come one day. The next afternoon he picked up his betrayers list and pointed to my name on top. Then he covered his face with his hands and cried and cried. I was a rotten daughter. I'd never loved him.

"After that, I made your father come with me. So Papa would have someone to talk to.

"A few weeks later, I was in the hospital myself and he was back in Lake Mohican. I'm not ready for this, I thought. My legs open. Interns, everyone, could come and take a peek. How resentful I felt. Then it came to me with the pushing that it didn't matter if I was ready or resentful, the child was ready to be born. That was the difference between Papa and me. Between men and women, maybe."

* * *

"Come quick," shouted Jake's neighbor. "You've got a grandchild."

But Jake refused to come to the phone to speak to his son-in-law, the man who couldn't hammer a nail through butter and the husband of the daughter who didn't love him. Instead, he went back into the bungalow and came out with a spade in his hand, which he carried down the dusty road into the forest.

A seedling came back beneath his arm.

After the planting, he washed his hands. "Bring up the baby," he called the hospital in Brooklyn. "There's something I want to show him in the yard."

"It was typical," according to my mother. "Why plant the tree on his property? Why not on mine? Why not say he was sorry, at least, for all those awful scenes he'd put me through?"

Nobody pointed out that she had no property. That she spent her winters in a rented flat in Brooklyn and her summers, after that pine got planted, at her father's bungalow here. Nobody pointed to the brilliance of my grandfather's ploy, the problems he had solved with that pine, the apologies and pleas he had avoided.

How unhappy my grandfather was when he found the first pine was a girl and not a grandson will be skipped over. He'd had enough daughters. For me his unhappiness had been a puzzlement. My fascinating grandpa's lack of interest in my fascinating being and accomplishments. Jealousy reached retrospectively towards my roots when the second pine he planted turned out to be my brother Jonathan,

golden-haired and bright blue-eyed, like Grandpa and the
Russian ballerina.

Like a toothless, stubble-chinned Rumpelstiltskin in an
undershirt, Jake stood beside my brother's crib. "He's
too good-natured. Why doesn't he cry a little? Is he re-
tarded?"

For only idiots, according to Jake, were ever satisfied.
Only fools were ever happy. To be smart was to be critical.
Then no one could pull the wool over your eyes.

The two pines before me now are more or less the same
height, despite the difference in their planting times and the
thin and rocky soil on this lot. "These things even out," my
pacific father murmured once, "in adult pine trees."

"Jake was mad for your brother." My father. "What a
smart kid. So quick. The usual. Your grandma had died by
then. His love, I'd say, was aggravated by his loneliness. He
dragged Jon around in that Rival dog food wagon. Jonny
hollering, faster, go faster, and poor Jake, he must have been
seventy something, would work himself into a lather. Then
he'd come inside and boast, 'That's some smart kid. Already
he's got me working for him.' "

One day Jonathan climbed out of the wagon and ran
across the road to the ball field to watch some bigger boys
play catch. Faster, faster towards the playing field, away
from Grandpa running after him in his old man's shapeless
carpet slippers. The old man stepped on a nail or something
sharp on the road. The nail pierced the slipper and the skin
inside, but Jake, who barely noticed, kept on running. Then

catching Jonathan by his skinny polo-shirted shoulders, he smacked his grandson's face. Two sets of blue eyes stared at each other appraising, astonished.

"I was surprised he cared that much about me," reported Jonathan. "Weird how at that age, I knew it. We both went back to the bungalow and kept our mouths shut about what happened. It seemed too intimate in a way to talk about, and the old man maybe was ashamed, chasing what he loved instead of running from it."

"He didn't say a word about the foot, of course," from my mother. "The toes cut out of his carpet slippers, I schlepped him back to the city when I noticed how much he was shuffling and they dangled his leg from the ceiling, dripping bottled stuff into his veins, but it was hopeless, he was diabetic. They had to cut the leg off by October."

"I still dream," added Jonathan, "of Grandpa chasing me. He's legless, with an ax. I wake up and thank God I live in California. Really. It was time to get out of there, out of that family. I made up the mountains here before I'd ever seen them."

Everyone has agreed that Grandpa in the hospital refused to see Jonathan, waiting in the hall, but no one knew why. Was the boy like Hebrew or that pine forest in Riga, something to flee from, and then encircle? Or something he loved, like his daughter or his store, that he threw away for fear of losing? His daughters entered the darkness of the hospital room and found the only light was a wrestling match on television. Gorgeous George versus somebody not so gorgeous named

Hans. "Turn it off," Grandpa shouted as he stared mes-
merized by two hulking bodies with their arms around each
other. Hair pulling. Thuds on the mat. Someone in the corner being sponged. Somebody's hand held for a second before somebody flipped them upside down. "It's so brutal, I
don't see how anybody can watch," Jake muttered as he
leaned forward.

"How he learned at eighty," said my mother, "to walk
with a prosthesis I'll never know. I saw him do it. Down the
hall towards the light above the nurses' station. The nurses,
they were wonderful women, cheered him. They held his
hand up like a champion. 'Get me out of here,' he muttered.
'There's only old people and cripples in this place.'

"I'll never figure it out. Did I admire his self-delusion or
despise it?"

His last instructions, written in a shaky syphilitic hand:
"Burn me, if I don't commit suicide first. No funeral." He
handed them to my mother, who obeyed him when he died a
few years later, as she'd obeyed in life. He went up in smoke.
My brother and I forgot him for a long youthful while, then
began in middle age to make calls across a continent to talk
about a man who was now ashes.

Nobody remembered whether he died the year my
mother cut her foot or whether Jonathan was in high school
then. Jonathan remembered my mother's cut foot. "I had to
cry to get her to a doctor. I was a boy in high school, crying.
She was diabetic. She could have lost the thing, like he did.
How many times, I thought, do we have to go through this
same story? Only there was penicillin now. Or some wonder
other drug. 'You didn't have to get upset,' she told me in that

little girl's voice she uses sometimes. 'Still, it's nice to know you love me.' "

I worry about those pines my grandfather planted. I worry about my mother selling the bungalow to strangers who look for the source of the darkness at the center of their house and find it, find them, lined up outside. A man arrives in a truck with a buzz saw and cuts the trees down, stacking logs neatly in a pile by the chimney outside. All of us will feel relieved for a moment. Jonathan in California, me in New York, and my mother flying between us, visiting grandchildren. Freed from something, blander, less contentious, more content, we'll feel what? Be what? Say what to each other and our children?

The strangers will sit, warming their hands at the fireplace, poking at pine logs to make the fire burn brighter until the woodpile is gone.

But now I get up off the stoop and start down the road to where the forest is. The road is dusty, but there's mud on the path through the woods, soft and then harder. Ruts appear and finally an impasse. Branches too heavy to lift lie piled, trapped between trees they've broken from in some storm, and the trees on the other side. I stand before the woodpile, listening to bird calls, then something thrashing through the forest — a deer, raccoon, porcupine or wolf.

Often after my father has said something that infuriates me, he'll add, "It's only words. I don't see what you're getting so excited about."

I've calmed myself by blaming the soldiers who criss-crossed his town and his tongue, dropping languages like pine needles for him to pick up, Russian, Polish, German, besides his Yiddish, Hebrew, Aramaic. My father, like my grandfather, uses words for what he knows already, doing business, praying, telling well-worn jokes. While for saying what he's never heard before, he takes to gestures.

But that animal is coming closer. I spot a place to put my foot up on the branches. Twigs scratch my palms as I climb up the pile, then stumble and pitch forward, sliding down the other side. My knees get banged against the stony ground. The dirt on my hands is damp and full of pine needles. In the darker, wetter part of the forest later on, I find logged patches, scorched places, scars deep as Riga in the ground.

Hair

"Got a hair story?"

"I have no hair story."

"Why not?"

"I get sick of coming here and talking about things like that. In fact, I almost feel like leaving when I get here."

"Why do you come?"

"It usually turns out I get interested. I told my husband, who had his seventy-fifth last night, the night before last when we were decorating the cake which I bought miniature candy rye bread for, what the topic was. He said: 'I don't understand how you can talk about things like that.' So I started thinking not about hair, but about how I could talk about things like that. But first I had to think about how I could *think* about them."

* * *

"I'll bite. How do you *think* about them?"

"Well mostly I don't or maybe mostly I don't notice when I do maybe. So first, I think there's nothing there, then I remember this and that, then everything comes back to me and there's all this, Ruthie, everybody tells me, you always . . . "

"I, actually, have been thinking about hair since the last time this group met. But really, I'm thinking about language. I went home last week and said to the man I'm living with, oh we had this wonderful meeting, we accidentally started talking about hair at the end. Now we're going to talk about it next week. And I could tell by the quality of his silence that he couldn't hear what I was saying. So suddenly I couldn't remember what we'd talked about here.

"So I started thinking about languages. The language this man and I are good at is like breathing. Our physical connection is intuitive and right. Not just sex, necessarily, but the language of what's to be done first and second. How to get out of the house in a rush and when to make a joke — We live together well. Yet it seemed there were a million things to say on this subject as long as I was in this room with you."

"I mastered that. When I was in advertising. You pitch your spiel to the least interested and the most interested guys in the room. And you keep talking. You never let the dead air get to you. Or you just loop into it and out again. Of course in my personal life, the bottom line is this: even boring people are interesting to me. How could they be that boring,

I wonder. How could they be interested in things that are so boring to me? But do they ever think anything like that about me? Not a chance."

"When you leave out parts of sentences, say things in a vague or general way, other — girls — you know, women pick up. Guys, at least in my college, they do very little of that, I've noticed. You have to talk in sentences that are logically in place and complete. Of course, my brothers slap hands and shout ALL RIGHT to say how happy they are. But that's at home. Or in the locker room or something. I get confused about all this, how people are different with different people and in different situations."

"Most of the copywriters I know speak in sentences. It's a problem, if you're writing dialogue. You have to rough it up . . . to sound like . . . whatever they are called . . . real people speaking."

"I hate complete sentences. In college, they always write sentence fragment, sentence fragment on my papers, but then once I started to do sentences, I realized that I, I don't do complete sentences well. They are invariably too long. Too — is it authoritative? Like some other century."

"Have you got a hair story?"

"You have no hair story, yourself, I've noticed."

*   *   *

"I'm thinking that maybe I'm thinking I'm going to have to get my hair cut. That's my only story about hair. Also, when my grandmother came to this country — she got married, you know, over there, and all her beautiful hair got cut off, which was what those Jews in Europe did. But secretly, she knew she was coming here, so she grew it a little under the wig. And when she saw that Statue of Liberty, she took off her wig with her children beside her and threw it in the harbor. After that she never cut her hair. Her hair was black and long. My grandfather brushed it. I brushed it. Everybody brushed her hair.

"Didn't you feel terrible, Grandma, I asked. Cutting your hair off because they told you to do it? She said yes, my little Ruthie, I felt terrible. I would never have done anything like that, Grandma, I said. You don't know what you'd do, child. But inside the house and out, she always wore a turban to hide that long black hair, so she must have felt peculiar, still."

"My aunt, the sister of the woman I visit before I come here, the one in the nursing home, always wore a turban. I thought she was bald. Because really, she never took this turban off. Nowadays I'd think that turban was East African, Caribbean, but this was Atlanta in nineteen fifty. Anyway, we had this box of photographs at home, which I liked to dig around in, and one day I found her in there, in nineteen fifties studio color — with this gorgeous skin and coppery hair, ringlets. Good hair, in the parlance. 'Did she have a sickness,' I asked my mama, 'or what? Hiding that hair. What's the woman's story?'

" 'Devra always *was* peculiar,' Mama said. 'I don't know. I guess she was saving her hair for the right moment. You know, all selfsame years she wore that turban, she had these Billie Holiday type dresses stuck in the back of her closet. Only me and a few others knew these things. She sewed them with these teeny tiny little stitches, then hid them away, would you believe it.' It stuck with me. My mama's story about my aunt's hiding these things. As a mystery. As the mystery, maybe. Along with the human race's meanness. Only there's nothing mysterious about that, honey, after you're maybe ten, eleven years old."

"I adore it. I had this grandmother who let me sit on her lap and comb it. I loved her for many reasons, but that was one. I used to worry because I loved for irrational reasons, but now I don't. I had a dream once about my ex-husband, who was something like this man I live with now, that he was standing on top of the stairs with most of his curls cut off. To play tennis or something. You didn't have to cut your hair, I shouted from the bottom. I felt so despairing about the difference in what we wanted. Now all the young women I teach look gorgeous to me, they all look gorgeous, they have great haircuts, I plan hair strategy based on them. Then I do what feels like me, which is Victorian."

"Do you mind if I ask you a personal question?"

"Not too personal."

* * *

"How come you were talking like that? About your mama and your aunt. I mean you don't, ordinarily."

"You mean, what my son calls, have that voice on? That 'honey'? It's because it's hair and my family we're talking about, instead of, say, medicine, or something on the work side of my life. My father, of course, my father was a college professor in Atlanta, and for a man of his age, a black man of his age and profession to use anything but the most formal speech would have been, well — he might as well have appeared without his clothes on. So me, I folks it up sometimes."

"Talking about uncomfortable, maybe this was only in Astoria, but I saw one of my younger cousins in rollers the other day and it brought back the whole — home perms with vile burning chemicals and then, how, for any special event, like one of my thousand sisters' weddings, we'd sit in some beauty parlor with poison dripping down our foreheads. And those dryers, could anybody turn them down? Not me. I'd just start fanning myself with movie magazines and sighing and moaning until someone came along to turn it off."

"We did everything. Lye, rollers, the whole bit. An eighteen-foot Afro, when I was twenty. That was fun. It terrified people. Especially my mama."

"Well, nobody saw me as anything, wild or tame or anything when I was a kid, but when I got to be a teenager, I thought I should appear. But when it came to makeup and hair, I couldn't do it. I was afraid to ask. Now at twenty-one, I truly believe my teenage years would have been different if I'd known — whatever it was, the other girls seemed to be born with. Also, when you were talking about language, I don't speak hair language. Layers and blunt cuts and so on. At the beauty parlor, they want to know in that language what you want them to do to you. My boyfriend says unless I know the language of each trade, I think all I can do is to submit to them."

"What else can you do?"

"Insist on something you can't describe. Or use pictures, from those magazines."

"My mother, from the time I was seven or eight, was absolutely obsessed about her hair. Which I now realize that she must have communicated internal states of being through, which I didn't think she had. My mother — not that I blame her, growing up in the most banal and horrible Irish poverty, will not spend more than twelve dollars for a haircut."

"Where does she get them?"

"Astoria."

"My mother, the only negative comment she'll make about people directly, is about hair. She wouldn't go around to my brother's house in Atlanta and say you dress terribly, but she will tell him he needs a haircut."

"It's funny. The only time I feel really comfortable speaking here, being so much younger, and everyone else has these lives and all these children, is when we're talking about mothers. Mine's hair color depends on the personality she's trying for that week. But then so does my roommate's. Depending on her mood, I mean. It embarrassed me in high school. We could do it, but not a grown-up. They're supposed to *have* a personality."

"My mother with the twelve-dollar hair might or might not have a personality, but she'll never refer to any part of her body as mine. 'I don't know what I'm gonna do with this hand. Look at what she did to this hair. Can you believe this foot?' "

"What does that mean?"

"This is the hand and this is the arm and I'm separate from it."

"When my mother was twelve or so, she got sent to Majdanek, which was a death camp, not so well known as Auschwitz, but with the same purposes and the same lining up naked to get your head shaven, which they did to her and all these other girls. Only her hair, which was black and thick and curly, clung to her and covered her instead of falling like the others' to the floor. She felt different, like God had sent a sign she'd be okay. If it were me, at that age, I'd think being different was a sign of — oh, trouble only. But then she was Viennese and I'm American."

"I never even thought about it — did they chop off my ancestors' hair on the boat coming over here? Or afterwards, on the plantation. And did important women in West Africa have special beads they braided in, that other women couldn't?"

"Of course. Everywhere . . ."

"I'd sure like some photographs. They — oh, make things matter. Like this. In Hiroshima, where I went with all kinds of doctors on that trip, there was this sign in this museum. JAPANESE WOMEN VALUE THEIR BLACK HAIR. This is the atom bomb museum, and the picture here is a woman with most of her scalp bare. I stared and I stared. Her whole life is ruined, I thought, no one will marry her and she can never have children. Then something American, tastelessly pragmatic but smart, came over me. Why doesn't she just forget her shame and buy a wig, for God's sake, I thought, and get on with her life and solve her problems?"

"I want to say, because nobody else did, about your — was it your mother in Majdanek, how terrible that was. And this thing that happened to my braid, it made me remember. Don't you love that? One thing that has nothing to do with the next, makes you remember it. Well, my mother had gorgeous hair and she saved her braid. I'd sneak in and put it against my head, to see if I could match it. Then my mother's friend came to town and said it was time Ruthie got her braids cut off, so we went to Best and Company. I hated what they did. My mother hated it. My mother's friend was very happy. So we saved the hair, the braid. For years we had that braid, but I swear it wasn't my hair, it was so coarse, they must have put some other hair with it."

"You see, Ruthie? You did cut your hair because somebody else insisted, like your grandmother in Europe."

"If you want to talk about compulsion, for a little while, when I was young, I went to a very tough elementary school in Flatbush. Most of the other kids were black. I had very long hair then. A lot of the white kids got beat up, but not me. Because I'd sit in this chair and let anyone who wanted to comb my hair."

"Was it humiliating?"

"Very."

"But why?"

"Because they wanted to and I didn't want it and I let them do it. Like rape, I guess."

"Oh, come on. Get a grip on your perspective. At your age, everything looks more — extreme than it is. Or, on the other hand, important things look like nothing."

* * *

"I was wondering why this hair grows. The rest of your body doesn't. Because it grows, we are constantly fussing with it, trying to adjust it. Plus it's the only part of our body we can adorn, without adding something."

"Right, you can't make your arms shorter."

"I hate arguments. I felt so silly when you reprimanded me. So I stop everything by wondering about things. Then I — I hate all that wondering. Especially when it's, well, fey."

"You want fey? My son who calls himself a Halfrican-American flattens his hair by pressing the top of his head against the wall in our hallway. And I'm sorry. You have a right to be young."

"The man I lived with before this one, had an Izro, this Ben-Gurion hair and wire-rimmed glasses, which made him look like Trotsky. I was teaching in a private school then. I had my long hair cut and frizzled until it looked like his. I don't know what I expected, but he wasn't altogether pleased. I did it because I liked his hair so much, I told him. He said, I know why you like my hair. Indicating because it was the texture of pubic hair, which was true. Then I thought, What am I wearing on my head? Everyone will see. But also he thought I was stealing it from him somehow."

"Is that why we straightened our hair? To not remind you of certain, shall we say, aspects of life?"

* * *

"My first husband, before he died, was very concerned, and I was very concerned, about his going bald. Oddly enough, my mother, with the hair obsession, didn't notice. Then the barber told him, It's okay if you go bald, because you have a nice skull, which made us feel better. As if he were opening up what was underneath instead of losing something. Aha, I thought, how nice. Then I thought, What is this shit? More advertising? Redefining things, as if that made a difference, instead of just — Well, he died later, so that colored my perspective. Death is like that. The language feels less and less adequate to make a — difference — afterwards."

"If you've got important news to deal out, the simplest words suffice, plus intonation. Take 'honey,' again. It can be kind when things are hopeless. Or cautioning, or reprimanding. All with one word and a change of intonation. On the other hand, hair, for me, these days, is on a different level. Something stiff and exterior like decorating your room. Or your office. I mean my hair is like my office and like my glasses. It's got to be businesslike and modest and so on, because I mustn't seem sexual or arrogant. Neither of which I'd want in a doctor. Still, some people are able to express themselves."

"I remember how my mother in Astoria used to say, It's not what's outside that counts, it's what's inside. I never for a moment believed it."

"It's not true when you're a kid. It's what you look like that matters."

*　*　*

"There were kids in my high school that had the aura of being good looking even when they weren't. Who cared what they really looked like? Another — ho ho ho — lesson in life."

"Well, for kids it's like, people who are tall are important. Or big in some other way. I remember thinking that someone with curly hair was like a curly person. That was the only information I had. So I made it have significance. Which if you want to be talking about language must be an aspect of one."

"Did you hear that — was it a car?"

"Some teenager. Peeling . . ."

"My mother says — how we all say things like, well, you only get one youth. Then she goes on to say that since she spent hers in a concentration camp, she made jokes with her friends, like girls anywhere would. About how weird their heads looked bald. Or that somebody would use them to wash his hair with."

"Meaning what?"

"That they'd be soap."

"I don't want to talk about hair anymore."

"I thought we were talking about language."

* * *

"I don't want to talk about language, honey."

"But the real point is: her seeing scribbled on a station when they were transported: 'There are no Jews in Hungary' and not knowing what it meant until the war was over."

"What did it mean?"

"It was a fact. There were none left. Just that. Well, I'll go on. My mother's sister who got saved from Majdanek by a fortunate marriage to a Pole, who had a visa to come here, was also a doctor. None of this does she remember, including the husband and the profession and me, her favorite niece, and her stepson, who never visits. What happened to him? she asks about her husband, when I mention him. He's dead, I say. How sad, she murmurs politely. Then yesterday, when I came in patterned stockings, she pointed and smiled at them, how wonderful they were, how happy they made her. Then she stuck out her hand and twisted her ring around, so I could see how pretty it looked shining in the light. Words go, but not adornment, apparently."

"Now I really think I have to go."

"Goodbye, Ruthie."

"Goodbye all. But first I want to tell you that my son-in-law, who's a psychiatrist, said these meetings are a form of —

group association, and therefore we had better be careful because . . ."

"I used to buy Aunt Hattie, the sister of that turban woman, because she was so vain, nice things, robes and wraps to wear in the nursing home, but everything, I swear, would disappear into the laundry. I figured they went home with the aides. Well, why not, they don't make anything to speak of, changing these old folks' diapers. There's a woman in there says 'five, five, five, five,' from the moment she wakes up, until they tuck her into bed at night. Whatever you're saying when a stroke hits, they say, your brain gets locked onto. And your tongue. The other day I saw her rolling down the hall saying, 'five, five, five,' and wearing Hattie's dress and that shook me up so much, Hattie is still, you know, human, she liked that dress and this woman wouldn't know a dress from a garbage sack, that I said, 'Why don't you say something else, for a change?' And I stood there in front of her chair shouting, '*Ten,* say *Ten,*' like a fool. I was so angry."

"I just don't know what to do. I always keep staying. Then I'm always late when I get home."

"Stay, we're almost done. You can always go later."

"On the subway coming here tonight, after I left that man I live with but couldn't talk to, I started wondering, believe it or not, if sex and being a woman cease with death only. Because I'd like to be some other kind of creature before I go. Then I started, all over again, looking at hairdos. It was five-ish. Those careful short-haired West Indian men who work in banks and girls like I knew when I taught in high school Brooklyn who are so beaten down, they straighten their hair, then leave it raggedy. Some musician, maybe, with a ponytail. Then this dead white older woman, whose hair was clumpy and shoe polish black wearing a lime green pants suit, nothing remotely punk, and men's shoes and no socks. So of course, I knew she was crazy. Not because of the socks, which might be practical if you're homeless, but the hair, which was something she did for herself, didn't go with the rest of the outfit. Anyone sane would have been classifiable, right? Which might be all I'm talking about. Only how do we know all these things? How to look crazy and so on? Maybe language is just what people say that other people can hear them."